The King of the Stars

THE KING OF THE STARS

BRANDON LAYNE

BELLE ISLE BOOKS
www.belleislebooks.con

ISBN: 978-1-947860-52-0
LCCN: 2019941523

Cover and interior design by Michael Hardison
Project managed by Christina Kann

cover fonts: Summer Hearts and BlairMdITC TT
interior fonts: Adobe Caslon Pro, Divenire, and Halfomania

cover designed using a combination of illustration and stock photography. Photos courtesy of @jeremythomasphoto (unsplash.com) and purchased Adobe stock photo #68038161

"The Western Hemisphere of Tashu" map illustrated by Emily-Grace Rowson

Printed in the United States of America

Published by
Belle Isle Books (an imprint of Brandylane Publishers, Inc.)
5 S. 1st Street
Richmond, Virginia 23219
belleislebooks.com | brandylanepublishers.com

BELLE ISLE BOOKS
www.belleislebooks.com

*I would like to dedicate this book
to my parents, James and Shelley Layne,
and my brother, Grant,
without whose support
none of this would have been possible.*

THE WESTERN HEMISPHERE OF TASHU

CONTENTS

1

The Richest Boy in Vennisburg

Brian Boulard was looking for something in his bedroom. This was no easy feat, considering its size. Brian assessed the room's various elements: its three large, pentagonal windows through which the early afternoon sun shined; books placed on a shelf without order, none of which would he probably ever read again; and several pictures of older girls (most of them wearing only beach clothing) he had cut out during his leisure.

"Where's that stupid book?" Brian asked. He quickly scanned his bookshelf and saw a lot of garbage he hadn't read in years: books about Day Kings and angels, mystical dreams and ghosts, ghouls and the afterlife. He took these books and, since they were just taking up space, threw them into a trash can filled with spoiled food.

His closet door was ajar, revealing an impressive assortment of clothing ranging from casual to some of the most expensive material he could waste money on. He did not particularly care what he looked like at that moment, however, for his mind was completely focused on what he was about to do, and with good reason: what he was about to do could potentially get him in deep, deep trouble.

"There you are," Brian said. The book he sought was under

a pair of polished dress shoes; he now noticed a single scratch that no one would have ever noticed on the side of the left shoe. He picked the book up and threw the shoes into the trashcan as well before brushing his hair and gathering a few bills. He never left the house without money or a brushed head of hair, in case he met the lucky girl of the day and needed to win her over fast—though those days, he had much more pressing problems.

A shatter of glass from below—it seemed to come from both downstairs and outside his open window. Brian ran out of his bedroom and walked quickly down the curving, elaborate stairway to the spacious living room. Glass glimmered on the floor beneath a broken window.

Brian opened the large mahogany front door, searching for the culprit. A small figure lurked near Brian's manicured bushes, his eyes cast guiltily aside. Brian recognized him as little Timmy, the boy who delivered mail around the neighborhood. Timmy's mail delivery uniform was wrinkled, his blue hat was askew, and his bag was bursting with letters. Finally, he met Brian's eyes.

"I—I'm sorry, Brian," the boy whimpered, his eyes bulging as they filled with tears. "They m-m-made me . . ."

"Just go away," Brian grumbled.

Timmy walked toward the next house on the street to continue delivering mail. Brian noted with no surprise whatsoever that the mailboy delivered his neighbor's mail neatly on the doorstep and left the windows untouched.

Truthfully, Brian didn't blame the boy—he blamed the two figures in red robes who stood several meters away. Brian didn't need to see their shady smiles to know that they had ordered the boy to throw the rock through his window. The Red Robes were just two of the many minions skulking around the town, making sure everyone stayed in line. They had large, italicized *M*s on their backs, and loyalty to their leader that would impress most dogs.

Brian walked out to his lawn and made a left. Usually this would be the end of their taunts for a few hours, but the Red Robes seemed particularly dedicated today. They followed him, keeping their distance, as if they just happened to be walking in the same direction.

In front of a house down the street, three more Red Robes were bullying a mother and her small son, but when they saw Brian walking in their direction, they left the mother. They approached the sidewalk, glancing at each other mischievously.

Brian quickly stepped around them, telling himself to ignore them and that nothing was actually going to happen—but then a rock struck him squarely in the back of the head.

"What?" Brian yelled, turning around to face them. Red Robes were closing in from either direction.

"What is it, boy? Rocks aren't your style?" teased Laurel, the Red Robe Brian disliked the most. She held four more stones in her left hand, and one was raised in her right. "Maybe you should have plants thrown through your window next time?"

"No, he looks like a fire type," suggested an older Red Robe to Brian's left. "We should go back and light his house on fire. That'll bring out some star power!"

Brian turned around, determined to walk away. But the Red Robes all closed in, pushing Brian toward the center of their ring, leaving him no way out. More were approaching from down the street.

"Come on, Boulard, let's see it. We know you can do astromy," cheered the nearest of them, chucking a jagged rock at Brian's head. Brian had to duck to avoid it. He announced to the group, "I bet you his watch that he *is* an earth guy."

"I didn't know you could tell time," Brian replied, ready for a fight.

One second later, he was on the ground with both arms pinned. The Red Robes were grabbing rocks large enough to batter his head, and one pulled out a lighter.

"I think it's time we helped you figure out which you are," sneered the Red Robe who had placed a bet on Brian's watch. "So, what first? Put fire on your fingertips? Tie you up and throw you into the river?"

"What is this nonsense?" barked a voice.

Over everyone's heads, Brian could see Captain Murray. Captain Murray was the least mean of all the Red Robes, but also the most loyal to their leader, and would never hesitate to use whatever force necessary.

Captain Murray's eyes surveyed the scene, resting on Brian as he struggled to his feet, then finally glancing at the book next to him. "I could have you locked up right now, boy. This book is evidence enough for Lord Mamlith."

"I was just going to the Flaming Café to read," Brian lied easily.

"Of course you were." Captain Murray crossed her arms and glared at Brian. "I'm going to let you go, boy. We've already arrested two people today, and I don't want to look like I can't control this town. But let's make this clear now: you do any of that *star blundering* in front of me, and it's all over for you. And I pray you have enough sense not to leave town. Those filthy malkin things have started leaving their hovels at night, and that'll mean more work for me if you get caught in their clutches."

Captain Murray walked past Brian and strode briskly down the sidewalk, back toward town. The Red Robes dispersed immediately, without a word.

Brian brushed dirt off his back and strode away hastily. These kinds of encounters had been going on for several weeks. More and more, the Red Robes had been attempting to push Brian's buttons, waiting for him to slip. One little "star blunder," and he would be in jail before he could utter a plea.

Brian walked down the street as casually as he could while looking around for any more potential trouble. The Red Robes seemed to have gone back to their posts around town for the time being.

Vennisburg was an average-sized rural town full of square houses with pentagon-shaped windows, set alongside a river that led to a bay guarded by even more homes. On the outskirts of town, a forest of pine trees that bore reddish-orange needles all year round was beginning to light up. Vennisburg was mostly a boring town, but Brian enjoyed how the Flaming Forest always looked like fall, even during the hottest summers. Clear skies, lush forests, and sprawling fields gave the town the quaint, peaceful feel of an everlasting autumn paradise. Even in midwinter, it never really became cold; the shivering of its inhabitants was currently due to fear of Lord Mamlith.

Not soon after Mamlith had arrived in Vennisburg, the scenery's beauty had begun to fade as he tore down part of the forest, set up watch posts, and turned the dense forests into construction sites. Normally a perfect reflection of the sky, the river had transformed into a bath of pollutants left over from the dictator's machines, affecting the wildlife and contaminating Vennisburg's main water source. Already, Brian could see machinery at work, turning Vennisburg into a tyrant's playground.

As Brian approached a factory at the edge of the town, someone walked around the corner, heading right toward him. Brian turned to hide, but relaxed when he recognized the figure ahead.

It was Malcolm Jones, one of Brian's favorite people. Malcolm carried a thick, heavy log wrapped in his massive arms, and a brown-haired bat perched comfortably on his shoulder. Brian was used to the friendly bats that kept Malcolm company from time to time.

Malcolm finally noticed Brian approaching and gave a great smile—something of a rarity during these trying times. Malcolm was in his early thirties and had come from the capital, Shohiro City, a couple of months before Mamlith had shown himself. Unfortunately, since the town's new ruler had forbidden travel, Malcolm was now trapped in Vennisburg. Nevertheless, he seemed to have made the best out of the situation.

"Morning, Brian. Why so down today?" Malcolm asked. His accent made it obvious that he wasn't from around town. Brian never could place Malcolm's accent— he sounded like he was pretending to be someone else.

"Take a wild guess," Brian mumbled.

"Red Robes again, huh? They never, ever bother me. Then again, I'm not a young boy. They know what would happen if they messed with me." Malcolm squeezed his fingers tightly into a fist while still clutching the log.

"I got into a fight with them just now. I sent two of them home crying, and the others got scared," Brian boasted.

"That's my boy," Malcolm said; but then his face became

serious. "Hold up a minute. Why did they want to fight you again?"

"They think I was doing astromy again."

"I figured you'd say that." Malcolm turned to shout to the woods. "Hey, you two come here!"

Two very large black bats flew out of the leaves. Their wingspans were as wide as kitchen tables. "Take this log to the edge of the street for me, please. Grab from the top. Thanks!" The bats obeyed without question and carried the log away.

"That's going to be me one day," Brian said jealously as he watched the bats obey Malcolm's every word. "Once I get this astromy thing under control."

"Listen, Brian. Don't go around showing off just because you think you're not being watched. You're the only astromer in town—in the whole region—besides me. Anything that happens will be pinned on you."

"I won't do anything," Brian promised, knowing full well that Malcolm would recognize the lie. "I'm just going to those woods over there to watch the pine cones."

"Alright. I'm going to find a place to sleep for the night." Malcolm nodded happily. "Hemo, go fly around and watch the Red Robes for me, then meet me in the woods in an hour. Let me know if they bother any more townspeople." Hemo, the brown bat, flew off.

When Mamlith had first moved in with all his things, a lot of other "things" had to go. Many people lost their homes when Mamlith coveted them. With nowhere else to go, they were forced to live with relatives, friends, or strangers, or even to find a spot in the fields.

What made Malcolm different from those people was the

fact that he still had a house. He slept outside because he gave his comfortable house to those who had nowhere else to go. Most people preferred not to sleep outside if they didn't have to, for that could mean crossing paths with Mamlith's night guard. Even now, Brian could see Red Robes exiting a nearby grade school. Three children cried on the steps as their old, cross-eyed teacher tried to hush them.

Soon, Brian was engulfed in trees, red pine needles occasionally dancing around him. He turned around, making sure he was alone. He wanted to make perfectly sure no one saw him practicing astromy.

At least, that was what most of the world now called the art. There would always be old-school saints and bizarre wizards who called the feats that Brian performed "miracles" and "curses." Of course, almost everyone agreed that the stars in the sky were what really determined the astromy one could do.

The stars in Brian's world were special. They could be grouped together to make signs or constellations. The way they aligned at a person's birth and how close together they were revealed a lot about that person, from their general personality to how athletic they would be, and even a rough prediction of the future. Brian had never quite understood how it worked, as there was a lot of math and physics involved, which Brian hated.

The moment everyone was born, their star signs and all the planets visible in the sky at the time of their birth were recorded. At age fifteen, students were required to reveal the star signs present at their birth before applying for their first jobs. Brian had two more years to wait before he took his exams.

After divulging his star sign, Brian would take his STARs (State Tests for Assessments and Regulations), which would determine what jobs and graduate programs he was best qualified for. For example, only those born under the sign of the Light Lion could become a saint, for the Light Lion sign granted wisdom and insight. In many countries, people born under the Shadow Snake sign were banned from running for government office, as they tended to be too selfish to lead. Many art schools still would only accept applicants born under the Earth Elephant, since this constellation empowered creativity and craftsmanship.

But Brian did not care for most of that. What he cared about was astromy.

The coolest thing about the stars was that they also determined who would be born an astromer, what forces they could use, and even how powerful they could become. Legends spoke of how astromers from the past could turn day into night, raise continents out of the water, command armies of animals, teleport through fire, or bring down lightning. It was even said they could raise the dead. However, astromers tended to yield the best results when working with the element and animal that corresponded to their constellations.

But the stars had changed as the years went by. They no longer glowed with the vibrancy they had in ancient times, and the constellations were becoming harder to discern. Many experts claimed that they were disappearing altogether—and taking astromy with them.

2

The Girl from the North

Brian sat down in the shade of a nearby tree and opened *Astromy Made Simple*, a book written by his neighbor, guardian, and tutor, Professor Rachel Chaff. Professor Chaff was an astrogist, an expert who studied how astromy worked. She had traveled across the land and lectured at many schools as a special guest, but since she only wrote academic books, few people cared who she was.

Brian read as far as the table of contents before he got tired of reading (because "reading is for poor people," as he would say when Professor Chaff published a new book). If impatience could be measured in gold, Brian would have been a very rich boy— well, considerably richer, anyway. He had no intention of wasting precious time poring over words he had heard numerous times.

Brian sat as still as the crisp autumn air. One thing he did believe was that hard work paid off, if only for those who had good looks. This notion was the only thing that kept Brian going after days with no results. He knew he should keep studying. After all, maybe today would be different.

Brian always felt excited when he imagined all the possibilities. Fire and wind had yielded nothing for him so far, unless he counted that time he'd made a match's flame slightly larger. He'd had some success with water and made no attempts with wood, because that was the lamest element, something only kids bothered with when they wanted to grow flowers. Today, Brian was going to try his luck with earth, the most solid force of nature.

Brian took a breath or two, and then pressed his palms together. Tensing his muscles, he pushed as much energy as he could into the earth through his hands. It should have been a simple feat: transfer energy into the ground and will the dirt to move before the energy dissipated.

For the first few seconds, nothing happened. Then, suddenly, a rush swirled inside him, his energy building. He kept at it for a few seconds, his breathing steady and slow. He pressed his hands against the earth even harder, until handprints started appearing underneath him. But the ground just stayed there, still and somber.

Of course, thought Brian. *At this rate, my astromy may never work.* Thinking he might just be lame enough to try wood, he stood up.

A cracking sound broke the silence. Brian turned quickly and received a face full of gritty dirt. Before he could react, he was caught roughly in the stomach by a rogue flying stone.

He fell back and landed hard on his shoulders, completely stunned. His ears filled with a distant ringing, so it was not surprising that he failed to notice the girl rushing toward him until she called his name in a heavy accent.

"Brian!"

Still clutching his stomach, Brian rolled over and saw the face of his best friend. Alasha had a thick ponytail in silvers and whites that framed her ice-blue eyes and long nose.

The King of the Stars

"Brian, are you okay?" she shouted.

Brian rolled over and tried to sit up. He had a cut on the corner of his mouth, but otherwise, he was elated. "Are you kidding, Alasha? That was my first time practicing earth miracles—I mean earth astromy—and earth actually moved!"

"You shouldn't be doing that. You know what will happen."

Brian brushed off more dirt. "We both know that if it ever snowed, you'd be doing the exact same thing. I'm always hearing stories about my father, how I *must* have his hidden talent, how he was a prodigy . . . I mean, how he was a talented man."

Brian had briefly forgotten his self-imposed rule of not using the letter "R" around Alasha if he could avoid it. She was from Touket, the land that had more snow than actual air. Whoever had created their alphabet seemed to have forgotten "Rs," and Alasha was not equipped to handle words featuring the letter R. She practically sang when she had to say anything with an "R" in it.

Alasha sighed. "So? You shouldn't come all the way out here all alone with no one knowing. It's dangerous out in the wild these days. And—"

"You're out here, aren't you?" Brian shot back.

"I'm looking for chanstones for my rings," Alasha said, holding up a glowing blue rock in a hand already covered in rings that bore the glowing stones.

Alasha had two main passions: furry animals and jewelry-making. She loved to make jewelry and clothes native to her home country of Touket. The people of Vennisburg loved the unusual colors and designs—so much so that Alasha's hobby had recently become a business, as she had many buyers interested in her rare Touketian jewelry and blankets.

Alasha hadn't been home to Touket in two years. When her parents had realized she was growing older and becoming more aware, they'd sent her to live with Brian in Kama, where she could get away from Touket's troubles and learn in a country that provided better opportunities. Usually, it was next to impossible for Touketians to travel freely due to widespread racism against their people. Their arrangement was only allowed because both Alasha's and Brian's fathers were very high-ranking in the military.

"I see," Brian said. Even though Alasha had been in Vennisburg for years, and even though they'd been friends since they were kids, Brian still wasn't used to her popping up unexpectedly. "Thanks for your concern, Alasha." He was back on his feet now, brushing the dirt off his hair, though there was no getting it off of his new, expensive sweatpants. "But nothing's gonna come creeping around here. Mamlith has this entire town on lockdown, and the malkins are out in the west or in the valleys. Trust me, we're safer out here than in our village, ironic as that is."

"Safe?" exclaimed Alasha. "Mamlith has his guards run around almost daily. How are we safe? And how long have you been out? Don't you know—?"

"Alright, Alasha, enough. But why shouldn't I astromize?" Brian demanded. "I'm not in the village right now. He said, word for word, 'There is to be no astromizing of one or more of any of the ten forces by any common civilian not under Mamlith's direct employ while in the town.'" Brian's imitation of the dictator was more mocking than realistic, but it did not amuse Alasha at all.

"I don't mind about that," Alasha said, stomping her foot.

"That man's bad. He's locking people away with no excuse, and you are the only one in town who can do astromy. I bet he's waiting for an excuse to lock you away." She went quiet for a moment before saying, "Sometimes, I wish all those things people said about the Day King were true."

"Don't start with the king thing again," Brian said wearily. He was tired of hearing the same gossip, day after day now, about what was perhaps one of the most famous tales of all time.

The stars could be read to see what kind of jobs people should have: artists, doctors, teachers, or military personnel. A person was often not allowed to become a veterinarian unless he'd been born under the Forest Fox sign, and many medical programs wouldn't accept anyone who hadn't been born under the Water Whamopus sign. Yet these elusive jobs all paled in comparison to the job of the person who was destined to become the king.

A long time ago, men had not become king because they were born into certain families, or wore fancy crowns laced with jewels. The stars alone had chosen kings, and these were true king of power.

The myths of the Day Kings had been around for thousands of years. Whenever there was great evil, a leader would be sent directly by fate, or karma, or god, or whatever elaborate word people wanted to use. People would know who this leader was because the brightest star in the sky, one that lit up the whole night, would shine above him when he was born, as if to say, "Here he is, right here! You can't miss him!" They called these kings the Day Kings.

"How long ago was the last Day King?" Brian asked. "Wasn't that, like, ten thousand years ago?"

"Two thousand," Alasha corrected.

"Oh, yeah," Brian said, recalling what he had learned in school. He thought it was weird that the stars were still used for assigning jobs, yet had not assigned them a proper king. The last Day King had died in glorious battle, and was now buried in some cursed mountain. There hadn't been a Day King since, possibly because of the long period of peace across the realm—a peace that ended in Vennisburg with Lord Mamlith.

The problem was, even Brian half-hoped the rumors of the Day King were true. As Mamlith's power grew, so did his ruthlessness. Things that had at first been punishable by a day in jail now could land a person months or even years in prison. The Red Robes had even let on that worse punishments were on the way, in the form of burning homes and being tied up in the hot sun for hours. As much as Brian believed fairy tales to be beneath him, the idea of a magical king at this point was starting to sound very appealing.

"Well, what do *you* think we should do?" Alasha asked sarcastically.

Brian opened his mouth to tell her what he was going to do about the tyrant Mamlith when a sudden swishing noise came from behind a nearby tree. "Did you hear that?" He leaned to the left to see past the tree. A quick shadow moved into the underbrush that was large enough to hide a spy.

"What is it, Brian?" asked Alasha, her voice low.

"That's what I'm about to find out," whispered Brian, grabbing a stick off the ground. He motioned for Alasha to back away.

"Don't be stupid. It could be one of Mamlith's malkin spies," Alasha whispered, staying close at Brian's side.

"I can take care of three malkins with my eyes closed," Brian boasted. His chest puffed out, and his confidence overflowed like a swollen river.

But then a growling snarl in the low bushes brought all of that to an end. Brian's mind formed one word: *malkin*. They had never seen one up close, and Brian was positive his money would not save him this time.

A pair of yellow eyes appeared in the leafy shadows, and Brian leapt back with a scream. The creature was faster and smaller than he had expected; it quickly zigzagged between Brian's legs and out of sight. Alasha shrieked as she jumped backward.

Getting up, Brian and Alasha stared at the familiarly shaped thing hiding in the shrubs. It appeared they'd been startled by nothing more than a fox.

"What a waste of—!" Brian began—and then he heard another noise and looked up. A shadow fell on them from above, and Brian thought wildly of malkins and pain.

Instead, this sound originated from a strangely shaped airborne creature. The thing appeared to be a giant bird—a real, actual monster with white wings that was going to devour Brian alive. It landed at a considerable speed, slamming Brian to the ground.

3

The Boy Who Could Fly

A quick white flash; then temporary blindness. The next thing Brian knew, he was on the ground, with pain banging inside his head like a loud drum.

"Ow!" Brian bellowed, one hand covering the right side of his forehead and the other trying to lift himself up. "What are you doing climbing trees? That hurt!"

Standing up despite the pain, he observed with streaming eyes the stranger who'd fallen on him. It was a boy of perhaps eleven, dusting himself off and checking for bruises.

At first, it was hard to make out many of the boy's features because of the filth on him. His jeans were torn at the knees, and his hooded shirt was crusted with dirt; clearly, no one had ever taught him how to groom himself. He had a young, round face; a thin body in baggy clothes; and short, dirty black hair with tufts sticking out. What Brian had foolishly thought were wings were probably the big ears that protruded from underneath the boy's hair. His skin appeared brown, but it was impossible to tell what was dirt and what was flesh.

The child's most unique physical feature was his eyes, which were deep wells of bright, rich purple. Brian had never heard of eyes of this color before.

"Brian, be polite. He's only a little boy." Alasha rushed to the child, grabbed his head, and searched for any sign of injury. An impact like that would have left a mark on anyone, but this child appeared completely unscathed.

"Sorry," the boy whispered quietly, looking at his shoes. He appeared to shake, sending dirt flecks everywhere. "I'm not very good at landing yet."

Brian was still massaging his injury, so it took him a while to catch the impossibility of what the boy had said. "Are you trying to say that you were flying? If you're going to lie, at least come up with a good one."

"Sorry, sorry." The strange boy grinned apologetically, revealing astonishingly white teeth for someone so dirty. "It was an accident."

With ears like those, I could probably fly too, Brian mused. This thought made him feel much better.

"Well, I think you landed on Brian nicely," said Alasha, smirking. She watched the boy looking around at ground level, peeping behind the closest tree. "You need to find something?"

"Fireworks. My kitsune," explained the child.

"You mean that thing that scared us to death?" asked Brian. "That was yours? Alasha and I almost killed the thing, thinking it was a malkin."

"You have a kitsune?" Alasha squealed.

"Oh, boy, here we go," Brian said, shaking his head. "Alasha loves animals."

"You don't understand," Alasha said hopping up and down. "I'm from Touket, and we see them often, except they all white, to blend in with the ice. The ones here are brown and red to blend in with the trees."

"You know a lot about kitsunes," the boy whispered.

"I want to be a vet one day."

"Fireworks!" the boy yelled, looking past Brian's ankles.

From underneath a nearby shrub pounced the animal Brian and Alasha had at first mistaken for a malkin, and which had seemed to be nothing more than a fox. At least that's what Brian thought it was at first, until he noticed that it had two tails. It ran into the boy's open arms, giving bark-like yelps. "I know! I'm hungry, too!" the boy said, looking into its face.

"Oh, I want to hold it so badly," Alasha said. "It's so cute!"

"That thing," said the bewildered Brian. "Is it some kind of crossbreed?"

Alasha rolled her eyes and brought her palm to her forehead in exasperation, but then answered, "It's a common kitsune. My dad and I used to hunt them because the teeth can be used in antidotes against poisons and such."

"I think we should go," interrupted the boy, still holding the kitsune in his arms and avoiding eye contact. "Malkins are close."

"Oh, no," said Alasha. "Brian, didn't I tell you? We in so much thouble."

Brian assumed she meant *trouble*; either way, he wasn't taking orders from a strange kid. "Hold up a sec. Alasha, how can we even trust this brat? *I* haven't seen any malkins. How does he even know this?"

"Fireworks caught their scent a little a while ago," said the boy, stroking the kitsune's head. He appeared a lot more comfortable talking to the fox thing than to Brian and Alasha. "He can tell how close they are by how strong the scent is, and he says they're around here, maybe four of them."

"Alasha, let's go back and leave the brat so he can climb trees again," Brian suggested, turning to walk away.

"I'm not lying. Fireworks says they're coming closer." The boy raised his voice in poorly feigned bravery. The fox with two tails barked harder than ever.

Brian was starting to lose patience. "If there were any malkins around, *I* would've seen them by now. They're not exactly the cleanest things . . ."

"Is that what you think?" A raspy, cruel, inhuman voice cut the air like a blade from behind the trees. Alasha squealed, stepping back. Brian was in shock—not least because the homeless boy's animal had been right and he, with all his wealth and resources, had been wrong.

"I'm only going to ask once!" the malkin shouted, cutting through the bushes. "Who's out there and what's your business in Lord Mamlith's woods? If your answer's not good, you'll never answer another question again."

No one had ever seen a malkin in Venisburg, but it seemed the rumors were true. Even Lord Mamlith evidently saw the risk of putting such creatures in town; they tended to forget orders such as "capture alive" or "return to the village in one piece."

"Crap," Brian said. "Now what?"

"Get down," Alasha said quietly to the two boys. "We have malkins in Touket, so I've seen how they operate. They like to be loud and in the open, so if we're quiet and low, they won't get us."

Alasha crouched down and led the boys away from the opening of trees as the malkins came nearer. She put a finger to her lips and crawled at a slower pace.

"They were here!" a voice croaked from the other side of the tree. The malkins stood where they were.

"They're listening for sounds," Alasha breathed. "Don't move until they do."

The three of them crouched quietly for a moment, until they heard the malkins stalk off.

"They'll stay near the main road. We'll go quietly this way," Alasha said.

They went three steps before Brian tripped on a root. He fell hard, all his weight on his left knee. A cry of pain escaped his mouth and echoed through the branches.

"We got 'em now!" said a malkin. Broken twigs sounded on all sides. There was nowhere to run.

"Get in here!" cried the boy, practically throwing Brian headfirst into a large, wet, decaying log littered with leaves.

Brian couldn't see anything, but he heard Alasha following suit. The log stank of earth, and worms squirmed over their fingers. Outside, heavy footsteps pounded against the ground like a frantic heart; Brian's own heart pounded against his chest when a malkin jumped on the log, shaking their hiding spot.

"Get them before they get back to the village," commanded a raspy voice, "or we'll never have them." Malkin chatter dissipated as their group broke off in all directions.

Brian, Alasha, and the strange boy waited silently in log for a few minutes, but the only living things that seemed to be around were the worms.

"Fireworks says they're gone," the boy said.

Brian took the kid's word for it and helped the others out of the log. The surrounding area look deserted, but they made their way back slowly and quietly, stopping to survey their surroundings at every tree out of fear of being caught. They took the long way around, getting back to Vennisburg in twice the time it had taken Brian to get to the forest.

The townsfolk curiously glanced at the new kid; in such a small town, everyone knew each other. Other than that, no one paid much attention to Brian and Alasha. It was common for villagers to stare pityingly and then walk away from people who were doomed, which was usually no secret since Mamlith's guards liked to drop hints about their next targets. As long as the villagers were only curious and not solemn, it meant no one yet knew that astromy had been practiced.

They reached Brian's house and entered, glad to be in a familiar place at last. It dawned on Brian that he had just saved two people's lives. A smile cracked his face. They would have been caught if it hadn't been for his quick thinking and superior survival skills. Seeing a potential problem, he turned to Alasha.

"Listen, Alasha. I know I'm a hero and everything, but don't tell people what happened this evening. Once word gets out about what happened and how great I am, they'll triple the rules here."

"You didn't do anything!" Alasha corrected, poking Brian in the chest.

"The same goes for you too—um, who are you again?" Brian asked.

The boy muttered something indistinct.

"Speak louder, kid."

"My name's Yenny!" the kid said. The beast gave three barks. "Fireworks told me to tell you that you're pretty." Yenny glanced at Alasha briefly, and Brian was sure he saw the boy's face redden, even beneath all that dirt.

"Aww, you a sweet boy!" Alasha said, pinching Yenny's cheek.

"That came from him, not me," Yenny announced, holding his pet higher. He seemed to crackle with electricity at Alasha's touch. Alasha wiped the dirt from Yenny's face on the nearest table.

"Okay, enough," Brian said, his eyebrows coming together in annoyance. "You can go now, before it scratches the furniture." Brian pointed at the kitsune as it hopped out of Yenny's arms and began running across the room.

"Can I have some food?" asked Yenny pleasantly.

"There's a dumpster over there," said Brian, not so pleasantly.

"Brian!" Alasha admonished. "He hasn't eaten in days, and he's sick. He hasn't bathed in months."

"He didn't say any of that," Brian said impatiently.

But Alasha had already turned to Yenny and said, "Of course you can have some food. I'll fix a late lunch."

"Alright. Fireworks and I will play outside!" Yenny said.

"Wait," said Brian. "Make sure you stay out of sight while you're here. If anyone comes over or knocks on the door, I want you to hide immediately."

"Sure. It'll be like hide-and-seek," Yenny said. The kitsune gave two barks in response, and together they ran upstairs.

"Alasha, there's no way he can stay here," Brian blurted.

"Brian, look at his clothes." The back of Yenny's shirt indeed had two sizable holes just below his shoulder blades. "Who knows how long he's been stuck in them?"

"Look at my floor," Brian demanded. "I just got it cleaned. I can't have that fox running around wild, not to mention the filthy kid. Plus, he's not from around here. If they find him in town, we could get in trouble. After lunch, he has to go."

"But just look at him!"

"I *am* looking at him. Did you see his eyes? He doesn't look like a normal person."

"So? He could be mixed with—"

"Alasha," Brian interrupted. "Mamlith's a kin-hunter. If he's mixed with any of those magic people, Mamlith will hunt him down. Haven't you heard the stories of all those heads Mamlith has on a plaque in his mansion from his prime hunting days?"

Kin-hunters were people who hunted magical beings, whether they were animals or people. The grand prizes for any kin-hunter were krystees, very powerful people who could perform astromy of such a great caliber, they could single-handedly demolish entire countries.

Brian went on, "I don't want the kid discovered here—for all our sakes. And I overheard some of the guards say that Mamlith might practice shadow astromy, so he could make life hard for us." They both knew that was an understatement.

"Fine, but I'm giving Yenny a bath first," Alasha responded defiantly. She walked off briskly toward the kitchen, but was soon stopped by a voice.

"Brian! Alasha!" Brian heard as the front door opened.

They both jumped. Walking through the door was their next-door neighbor, Professor Chaff. Her lab coat flapped behind her as she marched unevenly, a large briefcase weighing her down on one side. Her head was topped with a large Afro, from which three pens could be seen poking out.

"Hey, Professor Chaff," Brian said, looking into the older lady's eyes through her thick spectacles.

"The neighbors told me that you've been running in and out of town, causing trouble for the Red Robes. And more importantly, the librarian told me you still haven't bought my new book. Did you forget your parents put me in charge of you two while they were away?"

"No," said Brian and Alasha together.

"Good, because it's on my head if either of you get in trouble. So, what happened?"

"Nothing. We tripped while playing kickball," Brian said.

"Hold still," the professor said. She reached forward and grabbed a bug out of Alasha's white hair with her stubby black fingers. Then she fished a magnifying glass from her pocket to examine the little creature.

"How fascinating. You picked up a pine beetle! I can use this for research." Professor Chaff put the bug into a glass bottle filled with grass, then returned it to one of her many pockets. "Brian, you've got the rest of your life to practice astromy. How would I ever explain to your father that you got thrown in prison or worse? I'm in charge of both of you, and . . ."

Professor Chaff looked down to see Fireworks bouncing against her ankles. She then looked up and noticed Yenny, who had tried to catch the kitsune and was now frozen on the spot in the doorway.

"Hi," Yenny said, edging behind Alasha.

"Oh, he's fascinating," said the professor, pulling out the magnifying glass once more, along with tweezers and short scissors, from one of the many pockets on her lab coat.

"I'm fascinating?" Yenny repeated.

"It's how she says hi to strangers," Brian said. "Chaff, do we have to do this now?"

"A wasted second is a wasted opportunity for knowledge." Professor Chaff inspected Yenny's face and eyes for a moment, then lowered her jaw slowly. "Wait a moment. It can't be. Could you *possibly* be a . . . ?"

"Professor Chaff, the library published a new star chart," Brian said suddenly with wide eyes.

The professor gasped. "I'll talk later. I've been waiting for these updates all month!" she said, running out.

"That's the quickest way to get rid of her," Brian said, nudging Yenny. "She'll put a magnifying glass everywhere on you."

"I'll start lunch," said Alasha. She exited to the kitchen, leaving Yenny and Brian alone in the family room.

"So, is Alasha your girlfriend?" Yenny asked.

"Of course not," Brian answered.

"Then why is she here?"

"She's from Touket. Can't you tell by her hair and pale skin?" Brian said. "That country has it bad. They can't go a week without a war, people starving to death left and right. Luckily, both of our dads were friends in the military, and my dad managed to pull some strings and have her moved down here. It's way better here than in that crappy place, even with Mamlith."

"So, you and her have this whole place to yourself?" Yenny asked.

"Well, Dad had to go away for work," Brian admitted, half-considering just telling the kid to shut up. "I guess he's been very busy . . . . We haven't heard from him in some time. Professor Chaff is technically our legal guardian now, so she stays next door and watches out for us when she's not researching stuff."

"What about your mom?"

"Don't know, don't care!" Brian said quickly.

"I never got to talk to my mom either. Maybe we can be friends."

"Yeah, no," Brian said. He was relieved when Alasha came

back into the room, balancing three plates. "Hurry up and eat so you can go."

The three eagerly dug into the assortment of foods before them. Brian had come to love the native Touketian dishes Alasha liked to cook, but he'd never seen anyone eat like Yenny. The kid immediately started piling food into his mouth like he'd never been fed before.

"You like?" Alasha asked. "They're all classic dishes from up north that I bake and sell. That's halloumi made from *hippoverd* milk." Alasha pointed to the hardened cheese. "And here we have shawarma meat sandwiches, and *tahchin* for dessert." Alasha pointed to the rice cake mixed with yogurt.

"Wow, this is good. I bet Brian eats like a pig all the time when you're around," said Yenny, spraying food and spit everywhere.

"You just went through four bowls in seven minutes. *You* eat like a pig!" Brian cried. Then Brian remembered that the kid probably hadn't eaten a real meal in months. "So, let me guess: your sign is the Forest Fox?"

"How did you know?" Yenny asked, shocked.

Brian pointed to Fireworks. "You and that thing seem to have a lot to talk about." Fox signs were known to be highly empathetic and sensitive, to the point that many of them could command animals to some degree—although Brian had never seen anyone speak to animals as though they were people, like Yenny could.

"You're right," answered Yenny. "Are you a Falcon? Most people around here are."

"No, I'm the Elephant," Brian said proudly. "'Creativity and thinking outside the box.' Where you from?"

"The Woodlands," Yenny answered through a full mouth.

"What? You mean like Bosque Forest?" Yenny nodded. "Oh, man, I'm jealous. The Woodlands have so many cool places. I've always wanted to visit the Arthro Forest, filled with giant bugs and werewolves."

"Is what they say about Bosque Forest actual? That what you think comes to life?" asked Alasha.

"Of course not, Alasha," Brian said before Yenny could answer. "The Flaming Forest across the river is the only exciting thing in these lands."

"Why is it called the Flaming Forest?" Yenny asked.

"The forest is made of ember pine trees, so the pine cones catch fire at night," Brian explained. "But that gets boring fast. I want to go on an adventure somewhere like Miazu, where they have mountains whose caverns are filled with lightning."

When Yenny finally appeared to be finished eating, he broke the silence: "So, umm, what do you think a random group of malkins was doing out there?" He spoke quietly, as though he were afraid of waking a sleeping bear.

Before Brian or Alasha could answer, two loud knocks sounded on the door. Brian, who was closest, saw the outlines of several people through the curtain of his windows.

"What do they want?" Brian asked. He turned to Yenny, wondering if the kid was responsible for this—but he had vanished, along with his kitsune.

There was no time to wonder where he had gone. One second later, the door burst open. Laurel, Mamlith's guard, stomped into the room, along with the same group of Red Robes that Brian had fought earlier.

"Don't you guys have training or something?" Brian demanded.

"That was before we got the good news. We have a special guest coming to town tonight," Laurel cheered. "Here's a hint: It's not your dad."

The guards howled with laughter. Only one person would compel Laurel to casually come in and blatantly abuse her power without any attempts to disguise it. Brian and Alasha had seen this behavior before.

Whenever Lord Mamlith came into town, Laurel and her group would harass the residents more than usual. Several months previously, a group of Red Robes had gone into the home of Mr. Wilson, who lived on Brian's street. Mr. Wilson had complained of being abused by the Red Robes and demanded to talk to Mamlith, who was to arrive in town that evening. At that time, before he had been made governor and revealed his true nature, Mamlith was supposedly just a messenger from Christopher Cindoran, the Angelus in charge of ruling the land of Kama, sent to protect the town from the increasing number of malkins living in the woods nearby.

Brian had been too short to see Mamlith when the man arrived; instead, he'd seen a pack of Red Robes surrounding Mamlith like a human cocoon, marching in unison. They approached Mr. Wilson's house. Laurel gave the front door a swift kick; it swung on its hinges as they marched inside. There was none of the usual mischief on the Red Robes' faces; they were there for business.

"So, this is the house you disturbed me for?" Mamlith questioned, his voice effortlessly audible from the midst of his quiet guard. Several Red Robes stepped forward, took lighters from their pockets, and unleashed blazes of fire. Soon, the crackling of the flames consuming Mr. Wilson's house became louder than the screams from inside.

People had learned that day that if the Red Robes came to call, they should just deal with it. The faster the Red Robes got what they wanted, the faster they left. Even now, months later, not much had changed.

"Let's see. we need food, water, and some of these couches," Laurel said, surveying the space. She pointed at Alasha. "You. Massage. Now."

The guards kicked around the couches until all the furniture was in the positions they wanted. One guard pulled out a pack of playing cards; another started munching on some leftover bread from the kitchen table.

"I'm not enjoying myself, Boulard," Laurel shouted, even though her face showed relief. Alasha's expression was blank as she kneaded her fingers across Laurel's shoulder blades.

"Here's your bread, ma'am," Brian said. He hated to just lie down and take the Red Robes' orders, but he couldn't risk Laurel getting mad and searching the house—and possibly finding Yenny.

"That's acting like a good dog," Laurel said as she snatched the bread out of Brian's hands, shoved Alasha away, and jumped backward onto the couch.

"*Bark!*" Laurel commanded, staring deep into Brian's eyes.

The whole room went quiet; the only thing Brian could hear was his own breathing. He wondered whether Alasha was sweating as much he was; she was too pale to tell.

Biting back his pride, Brian gave a dispirited "Bark."

Then the guards let out a collective roar of laughter.

"I admit, *that* was pretty enjoyable. Do it again," ordered Laurel.

Brian barked as best as he could. It was hard work when his teeth were gnashing together angrily, but he managed to get the whole room laughing again. The guards cheered until the front door was kicked open.

Before anyone could react, Malcolm Jones charged in, bare-chested and sweat-drenched, knocking two Red Robes onto their backs. The other Robes got to their feet, but hesitated at the sight of Malcolm's immense muscles. Many of them looked as though they were about to bow to him out of fear.

"Get them," Malcolm said to no one in particular.

Five bats flew into the house behind him and attacked the Red Robes, biting their ears and scratching their eyebrows as the guards swatted at the flying animals.

"Is this what you guys get paid for? To show off in front of children?" Malcolm roared. "That's enough," he said to the bats. The creatures flew to the ceiling above Malcolm's head, waiting to see what his next command was. The guards stared at everything except Malcolm. Even Laurel didn't seem to know what to do.

"Leave now and do what you were ordered to do," Malcolm went on. "I'm not repeating myself." He cracked his knuckles.

The Red Robes all got up and ran out, leaving the couches and tables where they had moved them.

"Follow them and make sure they stay put," Malcolm said to the bats. "Let me know if they hassle anyone else. Hemo, you stay with me." The bats obediently flew out the door, except for Hemo, the small brown one.

"You just sent them running," Brian said with a mixture of joy and envy.

"Silence, boy!" Malcolm shouted suddenly. But he soon

realized his error when he saw Brian's indignant face. "Sorry, had a long day. Been chasing those Red Robes away from everyone. Anyways, few more years and *you'll* end up with these," he said, flexing his muscles. "You went around practicing astromy, didn't you?"

"They didn't know anything," Alasha said. "They just happy because Mamlith is coming."

"Mamlith's here?" Malcolm said in shock. "Listen, neither of you leave this house for nothing. You two are at the top of his list. This is what you get for practicing astromy. I'm going to take all the homeless to my place. Don't leave for anything."

"We can take Mamlith together," Brian said. "Why don't we double-team him?"

"Do you even know what Mamlith looks like?" Malcolm asked sternly. "He could be an astromer with even more power than your father. The dumbest of Mamlith's guards just made a fool of you. I am telling you again: *don't leave.*"

Malcolm ran from the house and shut the door behind him after Hemo had flown through. Brian just stood there, wondering if he was actually good enough to take on Mamlith. Then he heard a noise behind him, turned, and saw Alasha helping Yenny from behind the couch Laurel had just been sitting on.

"You!" Brian roared, pointing at the boy. He advanced, but Alasha rushed forward to hold him back.

"I'm going to kill you and that fox," Brian promised, trying to get past Alasha, who grabbed him by the collar with both hands. "You hear me?"

"That guy jumped on us," Yenny said, running to the opposite end of the living room. "You told us to hide, didn't you?" Yenny jumped up to peep over Brian's shoulders at where the guards had been standing. "Who were they?"

"They're employed by Mamlith. He's the governor, but he's really just a tyrant," Brian answered, his shaking slowing down a little.

"Oh. Is he nice?" Yenny asked.

Brian just stared. "I said he's a tyrant. A bad guy," he added, because the child looked confused.

"A tyrant is mean to the people he's supposed to help," said Alasha gently. "Great leaders help people, but Mamlith doesn't."

"Why don't you and your friends fight back?" asked Yenny.

"What is a group of villagers gonna do against his resources?" demanded Brian.

"I guess you're right."

In a defeated silence, Brian, Alasha, and Yenny began quietly cleaning the room and putting the couches back in their proper places. Fireworks was quiet for once, perhaps sensing Brian's fury.

"Did anyone ever try looking for the Baetyli?" Yenny asked.

"The Baetyli?" Alasha repeated, wiping the muddied wooden table. "You mean the Stones of Life."

"Have you seen them?" Yenny asked eagerly.

"Heard of them," said Brian, moving an ornate chair back into its proper place. "Alasha actually told me a little about them. I mean, I never understood why people think they're so special. I thought they were just magic rocks."

"What's so bad about that? Magic rocks are awesome!" Yenny said indignantly, his cheeks flushing.

"They're not just magic rocks," Alasha said. "The ten Baetyli are stones that manifest the power of the ten forces of nature."

"Which are . . . hold up; don't tell me," Brian said. After a moment he said, "Never mind, I forgot again. We just went over them with Professor Chaff in school, too."

"I think they're fire, wind, ice, water, wood, earth, lightning, light, darkness, and death," Yenny answered.

"That's good, Yenny," Alasha said excitedly.

"And the last one is supposed to be special or something?" Brian asked, growing bored.

"Death is the most important of the ten," Alasha said. "It brings an end to all things, so new beginnings can happen. Put all ten together and you have life. Still, there has only been one known astromer who was able to astromize death."

Yenny grabbed a bowl that one of the guards had been eating food from, but it slipped through his fingers and fell, shattering and spilling the rice cake everywhere.

"It's amazing that someone so young knows all this," praised Alasha quickly, cleaning the mess. Brian suspected she was trying to keep peace between him and Yenny.

"It's all thanks to my mentor!" Yenny squealed. "Saint Pa—"

Brian jumped out of his chair. He'd just had a sudden, terrible realization. "My book!" he cried, slamming a hand on the table. "I left my book in the forest, right where I was astromizing."

"Don't you even think about going back there!" Alasha commanded.

"There's nothing to think about," Brian said, pacing and wringing his hands. "They saw me with it earlier, but they weren't sure what it was. If they find it, they'll know exactly what I was doing. You two stay here where it's safe. I'm going after it."

4

Back to the Flaming Forest

Brian strode to the door and left his house, leaving Alasha and Yenny behind. He looked left and right before walking briskly down the road. He turned his head constantly, like an owl, making sure he was not being watched by Mamlith's guards.

He walked down the cobblestones, past the houses whose curtains were closed from fear. It was getting dark, so the only real light came from the scattered, flaming ember pine trees that lined the roads between houses. The only sounds came from a group of children who were laughing while running circles around the town square. The next block over, however, Brian saw a group of people who looked dirty and defeated: some young children lining up at the school, which now served as a shelter for those who had lost their homes to Mamlith's purges.

Brian arrived at the middle of the woods more quickly than last time. He looked around in the dark, which had settled eerily fast. The sounds of the birds had all but vanished, and only the crickets in the fields played notes, low yet excited.

The book was right where Brian had left it. He looked around again before walking out into the open. If there was anyone around, he might be able to scamper away before he was caught and associated with the book. But the surrounding woods were as deserted as ever.

Brian bent down to pick up the book.

"Do you know how miracles first came to be, young man?" came a voice.

Brian yelped. He turned and saw the outline of a figure that almost blended into the shadows. At first, Brian thought she was a tree; the woman appeared to be wearing a cloak of dark, reddish-purple feathers. Her eyes glittered, but beyond those features, nothing else could be seen.

Brian's mind froze, then raced back and forth like a cornered rat. He readied himself to duck and run if the woman made a move.

"How did you get here?" Brian asked, checking his periphery for the easiest route of escape. "Are you with Mamlith?"

"I serve no man that walks this earth," she said scornfully, as if she was insulted by the question. "So, do you know about how astromy began?"

"No, I don't," Brian said.

"It was the krystees," the woman said, though Brian couldn't see her mouth move. When he didn't answer, she went on, "You must know what a krystee is, young man. Or at least, what they say about krystees. Angels incarnated in human form, who descended millennia ago to teach us the ways of Theo." Every syllable dragged on, as though she wanted Brian to remember every letter she uttered. "That's what they say, anyway."

"Yeah, I've heard about krystees," Brian answered, relaxing a little. "Everyone says they're almost extinct, but I know that angel stuff is just a bunch of fairy tales."

"Really, now?" the woman said. "Have you not heard of the tales of how krystees can level continents in a single blow? How they can fly to the heavens and bring down fire from the sun, or travel instantaneously through space, or even awaken the dead?"

"It's fake!" Brian shouted. "My mom used to tell me those kinds of stories. None of it's true."

"You think so?" the woman asked, laughing. Even considering that she was in shadows, she was very difficult to see, as though she were half hidden by mist. "Then there is hope for you."

"What? Hope for what?" Brian asked, turning in defensive circles, thinking he was about to be attacked.

"Do yourself a favor," the woman said. "Beware the Day King. That's who I'm looking for, along with a certain item that could be useful. But then, I suppose everyone will be looking for him soon." A shadow filled the entire space. For an instant, Brian couldn't see anything, and then the darkness disappeared, and the woman was gone.

"Brian!" came a familiar voice.

Brian turned at the sound of his name and saw Alasha and Yenny jogging toward him through the trees.

"What are you two doing?" Brian said through gritted teeth. "You're going to get us all in trouble."

"Says the guy who goes into the woods to practice astromy," Alasha said.

"Guys," Yenny said, suddenly alarmed. "Fireworks thinks we need to—"

"Save it for later. Right now, I think we need to get moving," Brian said as he looked around again for the cloaked woman. "We're not the only ones running around."

"You couldn't be more right, boy," answered a new voice. "Do you think you can just sneak off to the woods this late at night and we won't notice?"

Brian closed his eyes in anger. Mamlith's guards had followed him here, after all.

The Red Robes surrounded him and his friends, blocking off all escape routes. Half had crossbows aimed right at Brian, Alasha, or Yenny.

The tallest guard, a tower of swishing red fabric, was the only one Brian recognized. Captain Murray, the leader of the Red Robes, stepped forward lazily and said, "Mamlith's been waiting forever to get you, Boulard. No astromy allowed in Vennisburg limits."

"We weren't doing astromy," Brian said defiantly. "So buzz off and bother someone else."

"Don't play stupid with us," said another guard, who seemed more malkin than human. His teeth were yellow, and his fingernails had a thick layer of dirt underneath them. He pointed his crossbow right at Brian's heart. "We've been watching you leave the town when you think it's safe and come back covered in ash and dust, carrying that book the professor wrote. And the malkins told us three kids were practicing astromy this afternoon in this exact same spot. You're all under arrest."

"You can't arrest us," Brian said, more outraged than scared, his rashness blinding him to the situation at hand.

Alasha's jaw dropped. "Brian? You lost sense?"

"I'm fed up. I'm not listening to these people anymore."

"Watch out!" Yenny cried out.

But Captain Murray's finger squeezed the trigger of her crossbow. Before Brian could give any kind of response, he was knocked off his feet by something solid, but small. The boy!

Yenny was so swift that Brian could not even comprehend how he had moved so quickly. It was just in time: an arrow from Captain Murray's crossbow whizzed like bees right through the spot where Brian's stomach had been.

"Well, what do we have here?" asked the captain in a calm voice; but her face betrayed surprise. While Brian was still trying to figure out what had just happened, everyone else seemed shocked, and a little afraid. "A live krystee, right in front of me. This just made my day! Mamlith always wanted to hunt a krystee."

"Brian," Yenny said quietly. "I don't know what to do."

A grunt distracted them. Brian and Yenny turned to see Alasha fighting off the guards who had come for her. Truth be told, she handled herself much better than Brian did; she punched one man in the face, stomped on another's foot, and kneed a guard in the stomach before she was knocked out cold with a giant rock to the head. Her feat was followed by some clapping from the Red Robes.

"The Touketian comes with us," Murray said. "Orders from Mamlith himself. Maybe this will teach you some manners, Boulard."

"Let her down now!" roared Brian. If there was ever a time for his astromy to suddenly manifest itself, it was now. He slammed his hands onto the ground, desperate to form a wall of earth as fast as he could to attack the guards and save Alasha.

There was a rumble, a blinding cloud of dust—and a blow to his stomach. Then there was darkness, and he was out cold.

5

Krystees

My head hurts, Brian thought. Even though his eyelids were shut, he could tell that the sun had set. He couldn't remember why his head ached, but he did remember practicing astromy at some point.

That was right . . . . He had been practicing astromy when Alasha interrupted him. Then Brian remembered the strangers who fell on him: a skinny boy with big ears and a fox with two tails.

Brian's stomach gave an uncomfortable lurch. He was moving. No—he was being *carried*. Had the attackers kidnapped him? He tried to see who was carrying him, but it was too dark, and his head was still spinning.

But his question was unexpectedly answered when a voice said, "Yay, you're awake! We can work together."

It was Yenny! The boy who was years younger than Brian—the skinny brat who'd supposedly flown into him—was now carrying him through the forest.

Brian struggled to speak, but he had no words to say. He looked around and saw they were still in the woods, though the sun had abandoned them.

"Put me down," Brian managed at last.

Yenny stopped abruptly and placed Brian on his feet. Brian

looked him up and down as more of the evening's events came back to him. The strange woman in the needles . . . being surrounded by Murray's men . . . and finally, Murray recognizing Yenny.

"You're not really a krystee, are you?" asked Brian, amazed.

"You bet," Yenny answered. He raised his arms as if he were trying to touch the stars, and the closest tree cracked and splintered as its trunk spun in a circle, the revolving branches showering them with red and yellow leaves.

Brian forgot to breathe for a moment. Finally he sputtered, "You're not touching them! You're astromizing the trees with your mind, just by thinking about it! That proves it!"

Krystees were even rarer than astromers. They were endangered, if the myths were to be believed—and with a krystee standing right in front of him, Brian was prepared to believe a lot. Naturally gifted astromers, krystees had supposedly created the art in the first place. They could astromize freely, without worrying about external conditions. A krystee could create his own fire, ice, or lightning from nothing, unlike normal people, who had to touch preexisting natural forces to use them. They were able grow plants in climates where it would usually be impossible. In addition, krystees were said to be perfectly fit: they had acute senses, could run at preposterous speeds, and were extraordinarily strong. Their eyes were vibrantly colored, appearing to glow. The list of their legendary talents was endless, and Brian felt he hadn't yet seen the start of it.

Still slightly in shock, Brian reached forward, grabbed the hair on Yenny's head, and pulled it back to properly see his ears.

"What are you doing?" Yenny asked. The ears of young krystees were different from most people's: pointed, oversized, and jutting straight out from the head, though the ears tended to become smaller and rounder with age.

"Why didn't you DO something?" Brian demanded as the shock evaporated. "You people are supposed to be top-notch astromers. You could've grown poisonous plants out of the air."

"I tried to help, but you told me to stay back, remember?"

Brian's hands twitched from irritation, but he had other things to worry about. "Where's Alasha? How come she's not here?"

A serious look crossed Yenny's face. "That's the bad news. After the captain blew you and your earth wall into pieces—" Brian grimaced. "—more people showed up. They were wearing red robes, but some of them had fancy black *M*s on their backs."

"Mamlith's personal guards!" Brian said. These were the men who had been following Brian around, making sure no one tried anything. If they were hanging around the woods, it meant Mamlith was already in Vennisburg. Did Mamlith already know what had happened—that Brian had been in the forest? Did he perhaps know Brian had astromized that day?

"I think so," Yenny continued. "They attacked us. They knocked Alasha out, took her, and left. They didn't even say anything."

"So you just let that happen?" Brian began.

"No, I didn't!" Yenny interjected. "I sent Fireworks to follow them. I waited a while, and then I grabbed you and chased after them."

"That doesn't make any sense. Why would they just take Alasha?" Brian asked.

Yenny suddenly became very interested in looking at the ground.

Brian grabbed Yenny by the neck of his shirt. "What did you do?"

"Nothing!" cried the boy, terrified. "Th-they might've, I dunno, they may have been looking for . . ." His sentence stopped short, and he dropped his gaze completely. "Me."

"They took her because of you! Is that what you're saying?"

Still averting his eyes, Yenny nodded.

Brian shoved the boy to the ground. "I knew it! This is exactly why I didn't want anything to do with you. I knew you'd be trouble! Great job."

"I'm sorry! Maybe they thought I was the king," Yenny added.

"The king!" Brian exclaimed, kicking dirt in Yenny's direction. Nearby birds flew away at the noise. "You mean the Day King? Are you joking? Don't try to point the blame; you know they were after you. No one's sat on that throne for two thousand years now. Even if the king was alive, what does that have to do with Alasha?"

Brian cradled his head in his hands in frustration. He didn't even know where Mamlith's guards were headed, so how were they supposed to rescue Alasha? If anything happened to her, it would be the kid's fault.

That was when Brian's mind started working. If the kid was who they really wanted, then maybe—

A quick shape came out of nowhere and butted Yenny with its head. Brian found himself startled for the second time by the two-tailed kitsune. It growled and barked in a sequence that was apparently comprehensible to Yenny, because the boy's face brightened and he said, "Good news. Fireworks knows where Alasha was taken. Some kind of new building where they have flags."

"It's Mamlith's new headquarters," Brian answered. "He just finished it a week ago. If they kidnapped her, that's probably where she is."

Brian's face hardened. He had to do this for Alasha. He had to take Yenny to Mamlith so the tyrant would set Alasha free. Why should Brian care about this strange kid? If it meant he and Alasha were safe, why did it matter if Mamlith captured Yenny and added him to his collection of stuffed bodies?

"Look, kid," said Brian. "I'm saying this one time only: I'm not saving you again like last time. That's a promise."

"Forget about me. We're saving Alasha first," Yenny said. This time he made eye contact, but it seemed that the effort was causing him pain; his face became sweaty and his brilliant eyes watered.

"It's not that simple, kid. If we break into Mamlith's building, we could end up imprisoned on the spot. They say he's an astromer like me, just not as good."

"We'll figure it out," Yenny said. "We have to save Alasha."

Brian was speechless. This boy could barely make eye contact, but had enough guts to risk throwing away his freedom for someone he didn't even know.

But it wouldn't be easy. They would have to break into a tyrant's home and face astromers and traps, armed with nothing more than their own astromic prowess.

"Well, don't panic like you did earlier," Brian said.

"I won't be alone. Fireworks is coming, so that makes two," Yenny pointed out, and Fireworks barked his approval.

"Well, we're three," Brian answered.

Yenny grinned, but Brian didn't return the look. It wasn't like they were friends or anything.

6

Lord Mamlith

ord Mamlith sat at his desk in his study, hands clasped under his hooded cloak. His face was obscured in shadows, as he preferred not to be seen. His desk was neatly covered in many trophies he had gathered from his kin-hunting days: teeth, hair, even fingernails.

Captain Murray knelt on the other side of Mamlith's desk. "I understand why you ordered us to take the girl," she began, "but I can't see the harm a child could do, even if he happened to be the heir to the throne."

On either side of the captain, giant puppets modeled after various people were on display, held to the wall by dark green vines. They seemed to be watching him, looking for any sign of disobedience. The yellow light of Little Moon that showed through the windows didn't help either; its light struck their eyes creepily, giving them life.

"Bring me the red-and-gold book on the shelf," Mamlith said from within the shadows, pointing to the bookshelf on the wall.

The towering shelf held many books of varying ages, but the one Mamlith wanted was titled *The Kings of the Past*. Murray found the book and brought it back to Mamlith, placing it on his desk on top of a map of the world, next to an orange crystal ball.

Mamlith flicked through the book until he found what he was looking for. "Read this page," Mamlith commanded.

Murray obeyed, curious. As her eyes scrolled down the pages, her mouth slowly dropped open, sweat forming on her brow. "My lord," she managed. "You have been given the wrong information. This can't be true."

"You of all people know that I am not a wasteful man," Mamlith said. "I have had friends in high places of power tell me that the last Day King was not born two thousand years ago, as we all believed, but very recently, within the past ten years or so. He was supposed to have been killed as a babe, but escaped somehow. Why do you think I came down here? To shake the commoners' hands? You know how efficient my spies are. By taking the Touketian girl, I am sure we will have forced the boy to reveal himself."

"But against this?" Murray asked. But, reconsidering, she relaxed. Surely those kids weren't anything special. A divine king should have stood out in a crowd.

Murray realized, too late, that her relief was all over her face when Mamlith said, "Don't underestimate your duties, Captain. It will be the last thing you do. If my plans are delayed because you underestimated these children, I'll have an addition to my collection in no time. You remember Captain Smith, correct?"

Mamlith pointed to the closest stuffed body. It was a lot less dusty than the others, as though it had been made only last week. It wore the same captain's robes as Murray, but its face bore shocked eyes and an open jaw that seemed to scream.

"Yes, Lord Mamlith," Murray said, bowing deeper still.

"Dismissed," said Mamlith.

Captain Murray finally stood and gave an awkward bow.

Then she left the room, closing the door behind her.

After waiting a second to make sure the captain did not return, Mamlith grabbed the orange crystal ball and set it in the middle of his desk. Scraping his heavy chair on the wooden floor, he stood and walked around the room to close all the curtains and lock the door. Now the only source of light came from the crystal ball, which glowed dimly orange on the desk.

Mamlith returned to his desk and laid both hands on the ball. Clusters of stars could be seen inside, a tiny version of the real night sky.

Standing before his desk and the crystal ball atop it, Mamlith paused to take a breath, like a diver about to plunge into dark depths. Then he said clearly, "Lord Elyon, this is your servant, Mamlith."

The stars inside the ball spun rapidly, until there was only darkness—a darkness so dense, the room around it seemed to have become brighter.

A voice spoke from the crystal's center. "For your fortune, Mamlith, I hope you have good news."

"Of course, my master." Mamlith fell to his knees and bowed to the speaker in the crystal ball, although he could not see the other man's face. "I did everything you said, and I may have found a contender. How should I proceed?"

"There are no contenders. He either is or he is not, and he only is if he has it. If he does, bring it to me, and the land of Kama and its people will be given to you for your services."

"But that weapon is too much for me to overcome." Mamlith tried to keep his voice level. "How can I overpower the Day King, my lord?" He almost had forgotten those last words. His eyes moved from the floor to the crystal ball.

"Von has already given you my gift to aid you, a small portion of the power I have at my disposal," Lord Elyon responded calmly. He did not sound angry, and Mamlith breathed with relief. "Not even Paleo will be able to challenge you now. It will be enough if you act quickly. Is it still glowing?"

"Yes, my lord, it is. He has to be near," said Mamlith. He rose and walked to his desk. He placed both his hands on the desk, and like a book, it opened to his touch. In the newly revealed space was a glowing, perfectly round white stone that Mamlith took and held in his hand.

The bodiless voice spoke again. "Keep it with you. It's the only thing that will give you enough strength. But remember to use it with care. Its power will be dangerous even to you."

The voice died away, and the crystal ball became clear again.

"Yes, my lord," whispered Mamlith. "I will not fail you." His breathing became smoother and more confident in the silence. And yet, even though his face was relaxed, his heart was consumed by fear of his master.

7

Mamlith's Mansion

"We won't catch up if we keep going so slow," Yenny said, hopping over a fallen tree and stomping heavily on leaves.

They had entered a section of the forest that was scheduled to be torn down for Mamlith's use, and the mansion was now clearly in view. It was the largest building in town, and Brian thought it looked very welcoming. Every window was filled with light, and the doors were decorated with gold latticework. If Brian had not known who lived inside, he might have been more eager to visit.

"Stop jumping so much. There could be malkins all around us," Brian whispered, looking from side to side. Everyone knew that malkins became less restrained at night.

Even though Brian knew where they were going, Yenny led the way; Brian was too busy arguing with himself in his own head. As the well-lit mansion loomed closer through the iron gates, it looked more like a tomb. Its giant gray columns were etched with constellations, and the lights from inside cast gloomy shadows on the lawn. Both moons were now visible in the sky: Little Moon, bright and yellow like an echo of the sun; and Big Moon, large and shimmering like a blue ghost.

No matter how steps Brian took forward, he couldn't stop thinking that this whole experience might just be a bad dream.

But the mansion didn't get any less real. Brian had a feeling that even if he and Yenny could get into the mansion, Mamlith's guards would appear the moment the doors closed behind them. He could see it now: the two of them being dragged by their arms to the room where Mamlith carried out his punishments. They were just two kids against many mean guards and malkins.

Alasha could already be in that room, being punished for the astromy Brian had done.

If Brian hadn't been thinking about Alasha, he would never have come so close to the mansion's iron front gate. It was now only steps away, and through the ironwork, Brian could see more columns flanking the main entrance.

"Is that his house?" Yenny asked quietly.

"It's where his guards stay," Brian explained. "Mamlith has never lived here. He's too busy talking to other governors and landlords, convincing them to work for him. He has control over all the mailroads, so we can't reach anyone for help without getting caught."

The kitsune barked at Yenny.

"I don't know, Fireworks," Yenny replied. "Brian, how *are* we going to get in?"

"We'll sneak in with these guys," Brian said, pointing to an approaching carriage. One of Mamlith's guards sat in the driver's seat, which meant the carriage would head right to Mamlith's mansion.

The carriage was drawn by a creature resembling a golden horse. It had green hooves, and two horns on its forehead. "I didn't know Kama had hippoverds," Yenny whispered in awe.

The driver couldn't see Brian or Yenny where they stood in the bushes, but the hippoverd stared right at them, lowering its head so close to the ground, it seemed to be bowing.

"Can you catch one of the wheels with wood astromy?" Brian asked.

Yenny held his hand out, and a wild root grew from the ground as the covered wagon approached, ensnaring one of the wheels. The wagon slammed to an abrupt stop, sending the driver forward in his seat. While he adjusted himself, Yenny and Brian jumped into the covered wagon.

Brian was thinking they might pull it off when Yenny tripped, thumping on the floor of the wagon. The boys held their breaths.

"Stupid straps!" the driver shouted.

For a moment, Brian feared the driver would come and check in the wagon, but the man merely sat back in his seat and drove on.

"I wonder what they plan to do with this," Yenny whispered, for they were riding in a dangerous wagon. What Brian had heard in town was true: Mamlith was shipping in all kinds of sinister things. There were barrels of oil, explosives, pickaxes, and ropes that could break a man's neck. The number of boxes suddenly made the enclosed space feel as cramped as a coffin.

"It's for us," Brian muttered darkly. "They've been stepping up their punishments. Maybe we can use these explosives to blast in."

They were silent for a long time. From the opening at the back of the wagon, Brian could see the stars. Astromers commonly had their stars read before taking part in a dangerous task or long travel, to help determine what their future would be. Brian wished he had spoken to Professor Chaff before he had left. She could have read his stars and seen what lay ahead for him tonight. On this night in particular, Brian wanted to know if he had a future.

The ride was quiet until Yenny failed to hold in a sneeze.

Not only did he sneeze, but what scared Brian was the fire that erupted from the kid's nostrils. If Yenny didn't get a grip on his astromy while they were surrounded by tons of oil and explosives . . .

Brian tried not to picture it.

"Don't do that again," Brian whispered.

"Sorry," Yenny said. "Hey, we're slowing down."

Soon, they came to a complete stop. The boys and Fireworks quickly hid behind the oil barrels just in case the driver came around back, but their efforts ended up being unnecessary. The driver got off the wagon and cooed, "Good, good. Who's a good girl? Yes, you want some water now, don't you?"

As the voice got fainter, Brian assumed the hippoverd and the driver had gone to the stable.

"How about it, Fireworks? Can you smell anyone?" Yenny asked.

The kitsune peeked out from the wagon and took a couple of sniffs. He barked twice.

Yenny turned to Brian and said, "It's all clear."

Yenny quickly followed Fireworks outside, while Brian followed less quickly. He knew wood astromers could talk to animals; he had seen Malcolm talk to bats all the time. But he had never seen anyone talk to animals like Yenny did. He spoke to them so naturally, as though they were people. In fact, at times, it seemed Yenny spoke with far more ease to his kitsune than to other humans.

Brian asked, "What are you planning on doing?"

"Get behind this tree, and get ready to run," Yenny advised. Brian followed Yenny behind the nearest tree.

Then Yenny turned to the kitsune. "Go *boom*, Fireworks."

Fireworks reared his head back—and breathed out a ball of crackling green fire that sped right into the inside of the carriage.

BOOM!

The wagon blew to pieces, blasting a hole in the side of the mansion. Brian and Yenny ducked farther behind the tree, and smoldering pieces of wood flew past them.

We're all doomed! Brian thought as they ran over the remnants of the wagon, toward the hole Yenny had made in the wall. Fireworks was the first to get through the newly made entrance. While the boys struggled over the debris, Brian heard angry voices approaching.

"Don't just stand there," said Yenny, already inside the building. Brian quickly jumped through the hole. Thinking like an astromer, he smacked his hands to the ground and covered the hole sloppily with a sheet of rock.

They were now inside Mamlith's mansion, in a brightly lit hallway that was currently empty. The boys quickly moved away from the wall, but stopped in their tracks as footsteps sounded from around a corner.

"How did this happen?" someone shouted.

"What the devil were you thinking, man?" asked another voice.

"My merchandise!" the driver's voice cried from outside Brian's sloppy patch to the hole in the wall. "My valuable merchandise!"

"To the dust with your merchandise!" said the other. "Take the fool and his beast and lock them away! Let's check the inside."

"Yenny, we need to move before they sound the alarm," said Brian.

But it was too late. A loud trumpet sounded from the center of the mansion, followed by a great scuffling of feet hurrying in every direction. The very first guards turned the corner, made eye contact with Yenny and Brian, and ran forth without hesitation.

Brian, Yenny, and Fireworks fled down the hallway, its stone floor covered with a red carpet so thick it was like running on water. The décor was lavish, and Brian would have enjoyed a look around, were he not being pursued with sharp blades and ropes.

The boys turned a corner—and came face-to-face with three Red Robes who had spears raised and eyes focused. The guards ran in their direction.

"Go boom, Fireworks!" Yenny shouted.

The kitsune opened its mouth and released three powerful blasts of fire, yellow-green, hot, and fierce. When the balls hit their targets, they exploded into showers of crackling gold, knocking the guards onto their backs.

"Great job! Brian, you okay?" Yenny asked. He had just noticed how far Brian had moved to avoid the explosion.

"Of course I'm fine!" Brian said. "What do you think I am, a coward? Let's go."

Before they could move, the situation got desperate. More guards had entered the hallway when they had heard the fireballs, bringing sharp spears. The boys ran in opposite directions. Yenny held Fireworks tightly, his shorter legs keeping up with Brian, who was moving as fast as he could. The Red Robes sounded as if they were mere feet behind them when the boys reached a fork in the hall.

"I'll go left. They can't chase both of us," Brian said.

In a blink, the fork separated Yenny from his view. Most of

the Red Robes went after Yenny, but Brian still had several right behind him. He scanned the hall, looking for anything to hide behind.

Brian made another left down a new hallway and nearly ran past an open door. At the last second, he lunged into the dark room, quietly and quickly closed the door, turned the lock, and held his breath.

Brian heard Red Robes whip around the corner and run past his hiding spot. Consumed with relief, he stood there for a moment, panting and wiping sweat from his nose and forehead.

Once Brian was once again breathing normally, he noticed a strange smell in the air: a strong mixture of wood, rotten meat, and rubbing alcohol. He turned around, more curious than nervous, and his heart may well have stopped in shock.

The windowless room was full of people—at least thirty of them, most armed.

Brian stood there, waiting to see who would come to take him first. However, none of the figures were moving. They didn't even seem to see him.

Brian noticed military commanders standing over a table. A couple was enjoying a nice dinner on a bench. Brian edged past the closest of them, and his nose couldn't shake the smell that reminded him of rotten meat mixed with sawdust. In a heartbeat, Brian figured out who these people were.

They were Mamlith's puppets.

Brian didn't know why he was so surprised. He had heard what kin-hunters did to people they captured. He saw all manner of people from near and faraway lands, convincingly lifelike except for the deathly paleness of their skin. They had plastic-like eyes that reflected the light of the moons shining through the window.

Brian had heard of the astromer kin-hunters who made stuffed dolls of unique races they tracked down. Brian did not understand the process, but he knew it must be messy and long. If Mamlith caught Yenny, the boy—or what was left of him—would be propped on this same wall the next week.

Walking forward, Brian noticed that many of the puppets were dwarves: short, muscular people. These figures weren't from Vennisburg; they mostly lived where it was cold, such as the mountains, deep caves, or the icy lands of Touket. Brian had heard that dwarves were the best sailors a person could find; they were the only people to have sailed across all four oceans and lived to tell about it.

Looking up toward the ceiling, Brian saw an impressive display of what looked like a merizen: a creature that was half human and half dolphin. It seemed the only group Mamlith was missing were krystees. Brian wondered if this was because Mamlith had never actually met one, or because he couldn't best a krystee in a fight.

One puppet, a particularly short dwarf with a black beard, was modeled to look as though he were reading a book. It was too dark to read the words, but by the light of the moon, Brian's eyes made out grotesque pictures of zombielike figures on the pages.

"He's into death astromy, too," Brian whispered, not entirely surprised. Death astromy meant many things to different people. Some said death astromy was the secret to living forever. Others thought it would grant the power to control the undead legions or summon ghosts from beyond. Not even krystees had ever been successful.

Brian moved uncomfortably through Mamlith's exhibit of the utterly still deceased, quietly making his way toward the largest doorway. He braced himself against the door and opened it, leaving the dark room and finding himself in what appeared to be a large greenhouse.

A great tree grew out of the middle of the room, its branches almost reaching the glass ceiling, through which the stars shined far more brightly than they did outside. Several large furnaces lit the room, but the wall farthest away was in complete darkness. A muffled scream came from somewhere high in the branches—a familiar voice that Brian recognized even before he looked up.

"Alasha!" Brian screamed when he caught sight of that silvery hair he would recognize anywhere. Her hands and legs were wrapped in thick branches that she hadn't a hope of breaking. "That idiot Mamlith put you up there, didn't he? Where is he?"

"I'm right here," came a voice.

Brian jumped and looked wildly around the room.

"By the way," Mamlith's voice continued, "that wasn't a very polite thing to say, now, was it?"

The tree's shadows seemed to split slowly in half like a black curtain, revealing a golden throne. A huge tapestry featuring Mamlith's giant fancy "M" hung on the wall above it.

Sitting on that throne was a man who wore a robe like those worn by his men, except with more gold tracing the hems and edges. He wore a heavy hood and a mask that covered everything except his mouth. Still, Brian knew that he was gazing, for the first time ever, upon the man who had cost his town so much. Brian also knew that he was in more trouble than he had ever been in his life.

"How did you . . . ?" began Brian; but he was unsure how to finish.

"A little magic will never do you wrong, boy. Though of course, you younger people would call it astromy, would you not?"

Mamlith raised his hands, and the shadows in the room pulled back to reveal several guards Brian hadn't seen at first, hidden by the darkness. "I can walk right beside you, and you wouldn't notice a thing."

"You're a shadow astromer!" Brian said with alarm.

"Shadow *and* wood," Mamlith corrected. He dropped his arm, and the shadows went back to their natural positions. "But really, that's quite beside the point. Did you think you could simply run around my humble house, even make your merry way through my trophy room with all my precious creations, without me knowing? Though I'm relieved you fell for my bait when I took your friend," he said in a singsong voice. "Do you like my gazing room, by the way?"

"Gazing room?" Brian asked.

"It's a glass room astromers use to read the stars," Mamlith said. "This special glass is made to intensify starlight and make the stars easier to read. When I was born, I had my future read in the stars. It said that I would be a mighty ruler, but also that I would be hated and feared."

"They got the second half right," Brian shot back.

"You think I asked for this?" Mamlith said, pointing to his own chest. For the first time, Brian noticed a ring on the man's finger with a ruby set on it. "I never wanted to be a lord, but you can't argue with the stars. They control our fate, our lives, and even our deaths. And so, I thought if I was going to be hated, I might as well live life how I want and rule how I want. You can't blame me. My sign is the Shadow Snake. Self-preservation and glory-seeking are parts of me.

"I don't like to waste time, so let's go ahead and discuss our options," Mamlith went on. "You can either answer my questions, or watch me twist and bend this very gorgeous tree however I see fit. It's your choice."

Brian noticed Mamlith was holding a vine in his right hand. Whenever he pleased, Mamlith could make the tree do what he wanted, which meant that Alasha's fate was literally in Mamlith's hands.

"Okay," Brian said slowly, his eyes darting between Alasha in the tree and Mamlith on his shadowy throne. "What do you want to know?" Brian knew what was coming. Mamlith wanted to know how many times Brian had astromized and lied about it. Perhaps he wanted to know where Brian wanted his puppet remains to be placed.

Mamlith leaned forward and asked a question Brian hadn't expected: "Tell me everything you have ever heard about the Day King."

8

The Day King

Brian had expected Mamlith to ask if he had been practicing astromy, or to demand to know where Yenny was hiding. Mamlith was a full-grown man with legions at his disposal—and he wanted to know about an old story.

"He's the king of the world, isn't he?" Brian asked, shrugging.

"Where did you find this out?" Mamlith pressed. "From books? From strange men, perhaps?"

"From books and school, I guess. Everyone has heard of magic kings!" Brian said loudly. What did Mamlith want?

"I see. And what of your friend? The younger boy. Did he ever mention the Day King?"

This, Brian had expected. His resentment for Yenny spiked. He was in the worst situation of his life, facing prison or worse, over some pathetic kid who talked to animals in his free time.

"I don't know," Brian answered truthfully. "He could be long gone by now. You can have him."

"My lord," someone called, and Brian recognized Murray. "Perhaps we should search the Boulards' house. If he really is the Day King, Boulard could be hiding it in his own home."

"It can't be hidden; it's a part of him," Mamlith said.

"What's a part of me?" Brian asked. He ran his fingers

through his hair and over his cheeks. Was there something on his face he couldn't see? No, that couldn't be it. He'd seen his face this morning. It was as perfect as ever.

"Perhaps I should hurt him," Mamlith said, with curiosity rather than malice. "It's been said the King's weapon's power shows itself during distress."

"What! You too?" Brian said. He finally understood what Mamlith was getting at. "You're a full-grown man and you still listen to fairy tales?"

"That was even ruder," Mamlith chided, squeezing a vine in his hand. Up above, Alasha screamed, and Brian saw the branches slither around her as they tightened their hold.

"Stop, you're hurting her!" Brian cried out, desperate. If only he knew death astromy; he could have finished Mamlith off right then and there. "No, I'm not the Day King. The last one was that Titan guy, wasn't he?"

"No," Mamlith said quickly. "The Zenith Star is the star of the king, and it's been shining brightly for more than a decade. The Day King is alive today. My sources tell me he is from a powerful family. Was your father not a gifted astromer himself? Power of his caliber is rare during this age, when the number of astromers is so depleted. Surely his offspring would also have extraordinary talents."

"Well, I don't!" Brian yelled. "I just came to get Alasha. Now let her go or I'll—"

"You are so rude tonight," commented Mamlith. He moved his hand again, but Brian had already placed both palms to the ground. It was time for astromy.

Before Brian could do anything, however, one of the tree's great branches came down with so much force that Brian was knocked onto his back. The giant branch rose into the air, leaving a decent-sized hole in the floor where Brian had just been kneeling.

"Did you just try to attack me?" Mamlith demanded from behind the creaking tree. He stood, and Brian noticed how tall and broad-chested he was. "Since your attitude is so impertinent, I know just the punishment for you." Mamlith turned and gestured to his awaiting guards. "You, go awaken the entire town and bring them to the stairs outside. You, go to the clinic and bring the nurses. And be honest; tell them I was disrespected. They will know what to bring. The rest of you can get started. We'll carry him out afterward."

The guards who remained went to the furnaces, placed their hands into the fires, and then quickly took them out. Brian was shocked to see that their hands were full of flames; they were fire astromers.

Brian knew what was coming and prepared himself to punch and kick as many of the approaching astromers as he could before getting roasted. Brian had attempted fire astromy before and seriously hurt himself, so he prepared for that same kind of pain. But he was too late to react. Fire rained down around him.

But not from the men. Fireballs in purple and red rained down from the ceiling, crackling like fireworks as they hit Mamlith's astromers, who shouted in pain. And down from the ceiling came a person Brian was both furious and delighted to see.

Yenny, followed by Fireworks, swung into the room and landed heavily. The men hesitated, looking from Brian to Yenny, eventually deciding the latter would be easier to deal with.

"He's a krystee!" the nearest astromer wheezed, only to have branches swing down and grab him by the ankles, hoisting him into the air like a caught, squirming fish via Yenny's wood astromy. The other guards were caught in similar fashions. The faster ones were able to avoid entanglement and ran to Yenny with their hands aflame.

Yenny didn't need Brian to tell him to run. He scampered quickly around the tree until he tripped and fell. At the last second, he astromized one of the tree's branches into his hands and swung himself into the air, just as fireballs landed where he had been on the ground. Yenny swung from branch to branch like a monkey, while the astromers below threw fireballs until their hands were empty.

"Kid, watch out!" Brian cried.

The branch Yenny was swinging on caught fire and quickly snapped, sending Yenny plummeting behind the mass of branches. Brian ran, knowing he was not going to catch the boy in time, and that Yenny would likely break his legs. But then he heard a ripping sound ahead. Brian wildly wondered what could have happened to Yenny that would have made such a sound. But what was that soft, rhythmic beating in the air? It sounded curiously like . . .

Yenny came into view, still in the air, and the whole room went quiet. Alasha's mouth was still gagged, but her struggling ceased entirely.

The first to talk was Brian, who asked in a scared voice, "Yenny, how are you doing that?"

Protruding through Yenny's hoodie was a pair of white wings sprouting from under his shoulder blades. They were very small and seemed barely capable of supporting his weight.

"There he is!" Mamlith cried out. He had moved from his

throne to see Yenny and was hunched over as though about to leap. One didn't have to see his whole face to know that he was greatly satisfied with Yenny's performance, not angered or fearful; it could be heard in his delighted voice. "There you are! *So* many people have been looking for you these past few months, and here you are in my own hall." Mamlith placed his left hand on the tree. Alasha screamed, but looking up, Brian saw that Mamlith had only moved enough branches so Alasha could see.

"Are you listening, girl? Can you see? I want you to see all of him. This krystee boy is the one chosen to be ruler of all, to sit on the throne of all the earth. The people of Mokan call him Maharaja, and the people of Shamland call him Ard-Ri. In the far north, he is Angel Child, and in the Mandalah, to the south, he is the Basileus. To the saints he's the High Angelus, and to his own people, he is the Stellarex. He is the Day King. The Prince of Power has finally been found!"

The guards gasped in fear. One by one, they ran out of the hall, screaming, before Yenny even landed on the ground.

Mamlith was still laughing, and Brian was about to join him. This was the best joke he had heard all year. This clumsy, poor kid a king? What nonsense.

"Did you suffer some kind of head injury?" Brian yelled. "Day King, really? When was the last time anyone has even seen—?"

"But Brian," Yenny interrupted. "I think . . . I think I *am* the Day King."

"You *think* you're the Day King," Brian choked out. In spite of the situation, he actually started to laugh.

"I meant, I *know*—" Yenny started again.

Brian had heard enough. "You're both lying. Even if the Day

King is alive, he's supposed to be a king. *The* King, sent down because these stars are brighter than those stars or some other nonsense. Why would it be a poor kid from the streets?"

"Why don't you ask that of Zenith?" Mamlith proposed, pointing to a particularly bright star right above Yenny's head. "Zenith is the one that marked him, and Zenith has never been wrong yet." Mamlith turned back to Yenny. "Now, why don't you be a good boy and give it to me?"

"Give you what?" Yenny asked, his faint voice barely audible in the silence.

Mamlith clenched his fists. "Every King has it. The final proof, your greatest power, your right. Show me and I will let your friends leave, I swear it. Just let me have the weapon."

But Yenny looked as confused as ever. "Weapon?"

"The Day King alone is able to wield a weapon greater than anything anyone else has ever created. A weapon created outside of this world. One swing can defeat legions of soldiers at once. It even bestows the power of death astromy, the power to bring back the dead. You can call it here, can't you?"

But Yenny looked as though he didn't have a clue what Mamlith was talking about. He still looked confused, but probably not nearly as confused as Brian felt.

Brian knew flying krystees with wings couldn't be real. Of course, there were people who believed in winged humans, but they were the same people who believed in a magical paradise in the sky.

Brian went through all the other common myths about krystees: they could fly through space, create stars, create elemental portals to different cities, and raise themselves from the dead. It was no wonder the Red Robes had run at the sight of Yenny's wings. If the wings were real, who was to say that a krystee, even this small boy, couldn't come back if you killed them?

Mamlith's voice broke Brian's musings. "You have the weapon, boy. And I am going to use the power of light itself to take it from you."

"What?" Yenny cried. Then in revelation, he yelped, "You found it! You found the Light Baetylus."

"The what?" asked Brian.

Mamlith paused, considering the two boys. "Now you understand. Yes, that is how I have established my hold on Vennisburg and spread my power so rapidly in so short a time. I used the Light Baetylus. The ten Stones of Life are the greatest weapons this planet has ever seen, besides the weapon of the Day King. I have cohorts all over the world searching for the Baetyli. With the Light Baetylus, I can astromize anything that its light touches, such as these puppets. Not even the great Paleo's light is a match for me as long as I have this. Once I have the other nine Baetyli, every city will know me forever as Lord Mamlith. I used this Stone to find you; it glows in the presence of those who are divinely recognized. You see?" Mamlith held up a beautiful stone so large his fingers could barely wrap around it. Maybe it was the light from the moons, but the Stone seemed to have a light of its own.

"I need that Stone," said Yenny, stepping forward, his confidence rising.

"I make you this offer," Mamlith said. "Surrender yourself, and your friends may leave my presence."

"We're not leaving," Brian said firmly. Yenny didn't move either.

"I'm not asking twice," Mamlith said calmly. He slapped the tree so hard he sent bark flying. Yenny and Brian had to back up as roots broke through the floor, revealing another chamber below.

Out of the shadows leapt puppets—not civilians or commoners like the ones Brian had seen, but warriors and soldiers. Their flesh had been replaced with hard wood, but their swords were the real thing. Thin roots attached each puppet to the main tree, placing them all under Mamlith's power.

The puppets surrounded Brian and Yenny, leaving them with no way out.

"Brian, what am I supposed to do now?" Yenny was barely audible. "I need that Stone. Can you go get it for me?"

"You're asking me to get the stone from him? You brought this craziness here," Brian responded.

"You're older!" Yenny cried back.

Mamlith's puppet army bore down on them. The puppets stumbled forward like zombies, their wood cracking eerily—or was it whatever remained of their bones that snapped with each step?

"Hold onto the branches," yelled Yenny.

A brief quake rumbled through the room, and then a group of small trees broke through the ground in all directions. Brian did not have time to grab anything; he and Yenny were hoisted into the air and toward the ceiling, tangled in the mesh of leaves and branches like flies caught in a web. The trees continued to shift, dragging them along, until Brian was caught in a tangle he couldn't see through.

"Alasha!" he cried.

"Brian," Alasha called back. Her voice was nearby, somewhere through the branches. Brian pulled and kicked, holding onto a vine in case the branch he stood on broke. Through a burst of leaves, he saw Alasha, twigs in her white hair and scratches on her face.

"Hold on," said Brian, grabbing the nearest branch to pull himself loose. Something long and shiny slashed dangerously close to his face. Soon he realized a blade's tip was mere inches from his eye. A one-armed puppet had been ensnared right in front of him and was trying its hardest to stab Brian through the throat.

Brian did the only thing he could think of.

"Help!" he cried, preferring shame to a blade in the face. He regretted shouting when Yenny flung a sharp and dangerous-looking branch in an arc through the air and missed the puppet completely, instead shattering the ceiling's glass dome and sending glass everywhere.

"He's useless," Brian said. "Get over here!" he ordered Yenny.

Glancing guiltily at the pieces of glass still sprinkling to the ground, Yenny flew over to where Brian was caught in the branches. Brian grabbed Yenny by the scalp and pulled them both beneath a dense canopy of leaves. Shards of the glass ceiling fell past them, crushing the wooden soldier.

Yenny looked at Alasha, crossed his arms over his chest, and then opened them wide. Immediately, the branches holding Alasha separated, freeing her. The boys caught her before she could fall over.

"Help me get Alasha down," Brian said. But the branches and vines they had been standing on cleared away, sending Yenny and Brian down. Alasha was a bit quicker and grabbed onto the tree. Just before Brian and Yenny hit the ground, long roots shot up from the floor and snatched at their arms and legs. Soon, both of them hung upside down. Brian strained to reach his feet to free them; though the boys struggled, it seemed neither of them could move.

"Last chance," Mamlith said, walking steadily closer, holding up the stone he called the Light Baetylus. It was glowing even brighter than before. "Give me the weapon, and I'll let your friends go."

"Yenny, give him what he wants!" Brian said. Right below him—or, since he was upside down, above him—what remained of Mamlith's waiting wooden army was still and broken as if they had all died again.

"I don't have a weapon!" Yenny said. "What does it look like?"

"Say farewell, Brian," Mamlith said. He squeezed the closest branch, and the whole tree shook. Brian was lowered slowly to the mass of puppets, who started hacking at the air with their swords.

"I don't have it! I don't have it! I don't have it!" Yenny repeated.

"You mean to tell me it's truly not here? You're telling the truth?" Mamlith screamed. He let go of the branch, and both Brian and the puppets stopped moving. Brian kicked at the nearest wooden soldier.

"So you are indeed *not* the Day King," Mamlith said, the corners of his mouth turning down in disappointment.

If his blood hadn't been rushing to his head, Brian might have felt sorry for Mamlith. He wondered how long the man had practiced his dramatic speech in front of a mirror for this moment.

"Yes, I am," Yenny said, struggling against his bonds.

"No, you are not," Mamlith said. If Brian hadn't known

better, he would have sworn that Mamlith sounded truly hurt and lost. "I was *sure* you were him; I dreamed of this." Mamlith cursed to himself, which gave Brian enough time to look up. Several dozen feet above him and Yenny, Alasha, forgotten by Mamlith, was silently moving a broken branch.

"At least," Mamlith said, "I still have the opportunity to do *this*." He raised the Stone and pointed it at Yenny. The light inside began to glow brighter.

But whatever Mamlith intended to do never happened. Instead, Alasha dropped the huge, broken limb over the tyrant's head.

Mamlith yelled in pain as he stumbled, his free hand clutching his forehead. He dropped the Stone to clutch his throbbing head.

Brian broke from his restraints and half jumped, half climbed to the floor, which was now covered in broken branches and bent weapons. He sprinted and grabbed the Stone just as Mamlith steadied himself.

Mamlith leapt forward with a great cry. The tree bent under Yenny's power, latching its branches around Mamlith.

Mamlith's angry scream was drowned out by the others' cheers.

9

Victory

They had done what most adults could not. Brian helped Alasha climb down the tree. Together, they ran to untangle Yenny from the puppets' strings.

They stood in shock, not believing what had just happened. Mamlith's arms were bound tightly in the tree's branches, preventing him from astromizing. His mask still covered most of his face.

Brian was the first to break the silence.

"Did you see what we did?" Brian asked. "Let's tell everyone and celebrate. We'll have a party thrown for us."

"Let's get food! Lots of it!" Yenny said. He tripped on a root as he walked over to them.

"You're hurt!" Alasha said.

"No, I'm not," Yenny said. "I just slipped on a string."

"You going to the clinic," Alasha said firmly. "I'll help you walk. I think you twisted ankle."

"He's not going anywhere until I tell everyone that everything that happened to the town was his fault," Brian said. "Mamlith clearly came to town looking for him. I was thrown to the ground, had rocks thrown at me—and you," he said, turning to the defeated Mamlith. "I hope you feel real stupid right now, thinking he was the Day King."

"Yes, yes," said Mamlith, still trapped in his cocoon of branches. "A foolish mistake. Day Kings were mighty, and you would have had the weapon. Not that it matters now. I've still won."

"Ha!" Brian said. Feeling a lot braver now, he walked up to Mamlith, waving the white Stone right in front of his eyes. "And how are you going to take this from us now?"

"Did you forget that I'm a wood astromer?" Mamlith asked.

It took a moment for the kids to process what he'd said, but Mamlith had already freed himself from his bonds and stooped to touch the nearest root. A branch quickly entangled Brian's arm like a snake, forcing him to drop the Stone into Mamlith's open palm. A white light suddenly blazed, blinding everyone. Brian heard Yenny trip onto Alasha in the chaos. He could just make out white light pouring out of Mamlith's eyes, nostrils, and mouth.

And then Mamlith screamed in agony and clutched one hand with the other. "No, no, no!" Mamlith's voice sliced through the blinding light. "I used its power before. Why is it rejecting me now?" Mamlith cursed as he gave one final cry before the Light Baetylus exploded with light, blasting Yenny, Brian, and Alasha off their feet.

It sounded like the whole building was collapsing, though Brian was still too blind to see anything. Brian grabbed Alasha's hand as crashes sounded all around them, the floor thundering so badly they couldn't even crawl away.

The light dimmed slowly, bringing Yenny into view. He was standing over them with his arms outstretched—he had summoned a barrage of roots to protect them from the collapsing ceiling and obliterated tree. The room quivered and quaked around them, rumbling and thundering—until at last, it all fell silent.

"What happened?" asked Alasha. Dust and leaves were everywhere, and voices shouted from the other side of the collapsed wall. Brian had forgotten that the Red Robes had been sent to gather the townsfolk to witness his punishment. Looking up in desperation, Brian could see the Big Moon clearly through the crumbled ceiling overhead.

"Yenny, don't!" Alasha said.

Yenny ignored her, spread his wings, and fluttered over the rubble and broken trees. He picked something up off the floor, then flew back down. Brian saw that Yenny clutched the same jewel that Mamlith had just used, still glowing with its mystical white light.

A great distance away, Lord Elyon stood on the roof of a tall tower in the middle of a black castle, gazing up at the stars spattered across the midnight sky while rubbing a round black stone between his fingers. A second man, Von, stood behind Lord Elyon at a respectful distance while Elyon read the stars. Both men wore black robes and hoods, but Von also wore a white mask, behind which a pair of bright yellow eyes shone.

"Lord Elyon! The Baetylus?" Von called.

Elyon looked at the perfectly spherical black stone in his hand, and saw that it was shaking. Holding it up against the stars, he peered into it.

"Just as I suspected," Lord Elyon said at last. "Mamlith is with us no more, Von. His lust for power has been his undoing, it seems."

"So he tried to use the Light Baetylus while—?"

"Yes, the fool. He should have known that using the Stone recklessly would bear ill for him. It is a shame to lose such a valuable ally, but we have a more important problem. The Orb of Light is most likely no longer in our possession."

"I have failed." Von averted his gaze from Elyon's, instead watching the black stone shaking in Elyon's hands. "I was the one who chose Mamlith. I believed he was a man dedicated to our cause!"

"You are not to blame," Elyon said sharply. "You have performed marvelously in the past, and still do. Your lord is a merciful lord."

"Yes, indeed," said Von.

"Say it," Lord Elyon demanded. "He wants to hear you say it." The shadows across the roof deepened and slithered outward like serpents as Von's master grew impatient.

"My—my lord is merciful and righteous," Von spoke. The shadows coiled back to their corners, and Von let out a long, deep breath. "So, you believe the Day King possesses it now, my lord?"

"It is very likely," Lord Elyon began. "But we must look at the possible consequences; this can be either good or bad for our cause. If the Day King is truly at the root of this, he may go after all of the Baetyli for us. We need to send someone after the Light Baetylus and find the one who made Mamlith throw caution to the winds."

"If my lord commands it of me, it shall be done at once!" Von proclaimed. The yellow in his eyes flashed even more brightly.

"That would be most unwise, Von," Elyon said. "You have magnificent abilities, but they need to stay hidden a little longer. I have someone else in mind . . ."

10

The Dark Cellar

When Brian, Alasha, and Yenny finally emerged from the rubble of Mamlith's manor, the whole town was waiting for them. People ran forward to help them out of the rubble, giving Yenny suspicious sideways glances.

Every variant of "What happened?" was asked. Brian did his best to convey what had happened: the Red Robes had captured Alasha; Brian had followed, broken into the mansion, and been captured; and then, at the last moment, the two had been saved.

Everyone asked about the guardian or soldier who had done this heroic thing. Instead, they were presented with a small, skinny child who looked as though he was about to faint.

"He's a krystee!" Professor Chaff said, pulling Yenny forward. "Notice the angles of his ears and the coloring of his eyes. If you read my book—"

"What gave you the courage to do all of this, young man?" interrupted an older lady.

"I'm the King," Yenny whispered, barely audible to Brian from this close distance.

"Uh, of what?" asked a woman.

"I'm the Day King," Yenny said.

"You mean the, er, the actual Day King?"

The crowd went quiet for a moment, then erupted into laughter and applause.

"That's just adorable," Professor Chaff said, patting Yenny on the shoulder. "Well, you'd be the best king I've ever met."

"But I am," Yenny whined.

"There are no such things as Day Kings," Professor Chaff said firmly. "They're just myths."

"Ah, let him have it!" someone yelled from the crowd. There was another round of cheers.

"But what if he is?" Alasha asked the professor quietly. "Mamlith said something about a weapon that only the Day King can use."

"Ah, yes," said Professor Chaff. "*That*. That's not important. It's just a very expensive souvenir."

"What is it?" Brian asked, enticed by the words "very expensive."

"A fabled object from an ancient time. We scientists discount that nonsense as random ties people use to bridge the gaps in our historic evolution. Now, if you're interested in hearing about the new thesis I've been developing—"

"Alasha would love to," Brian said, disappearing into the crowd just as the professor turned to the furious Alasha.

And that was how Yenny's fame in Vennisburg all started. From that day on, elderly men shook Yenny's hand on the street, young women bestowed rib-cracking hugs without warning, and young children stared with their mouths hanging open.

When they found out Yenny was homeless, practically everyone offered to open their homes to him. In the end, Yenny decided to stay in the motel that stood in the market square. The townsfolk ushered him into the luxury suite and brought him three meals a day, refusing payment.

Meanwhile, they began searching through Mamlith's collapsed mansion to see if there was anything worth finding. Yenny and Alasha joined Professor Chaff on one of these trips to see if there was anything interesting to study. Outside the crumbled building, many people were inspecting golden treasures they had found. Professor Chaff alone found the dirty, crumbling vases and fossils fascinating.

"Such fascinating charts," Professor Chaff said, poring over some ancient-looking parchment. "The star charts are showing stars formations we haven't seen in years. I wonder what kind of futures have been predicted."

"Look at what Alasha and I found," Yenny said. He showed Professor Chaff a crystal ball filled with stars.

"That's an Elven Eye," Professor Chaff said. "It's said that saints and mages use them to see things far away. But I never heard of one actually working."

"You never heard of one working?" Yenny repeated.

"Yes," Professor Chaff confirmed. "They're strangely temperamental, and they rarely activate when they're supposed to."

Yenny shrugged, tucking the object into his pocket. "Still, it looks cool! I'm keeping it anyway."

"Yenny, is that you?" Alasha asked.

Yenny turned around, and his face reddened. One of Yenny's fans had a giant drawing of Yenny's head and was waving it around on the end of a wooden fence post. The children only knew it was him because of the krystee wings coming from the back, but otherwise the picture could have been him.

For weeks, people continued to celebrate across the bay.

They no longer feared being locked away for reasons like smiling and laughing. The best part was that the Red Robes were gone. Without Mamlith backing them up, they didn't have the courage to continue to bully the town. Many of the townsfolk found the Red Robes and ran after them with shovels and sticks. The Red Robes who ran the slowest got shovels to the face and sticks to the back, limping their way out of Vennisburg.

Unfortunately, not everything was well.

About a month after Alasha's rescue, Professor Chaff walked into Brian's house. "I have bad news, everyone," she said, in a slow, low voice. Alasha looked up from the stove, where she had been teaching Yenny how to cook various Touketian dishes. "We found someone buried in the rubble."

"It's Mamlith, isn't it?" Alasha asked.

"No. We haven't found any trace of him yet. He's likely been crushed. But perhaps you should come with me to the clinic."

"The clinic?" Brian asked. "Why?"

"Who's hurt?" Alasha demanded.

But Professor Chaff refused to give any more details, so, arguing amongst themselves, they all walked outside toward the nurse's clinic.

It would have been a relatively short walk even without all the people stopping to talk to and congratulate them. When they finally entered the clinic, Brian saw beds with nice, clean linens lined up against the wall. Patients of all ages were bundled up in bandages and blankets, and many of the beds were occupied. Nurses tended to the injured while medicists—people trained to heal those who were sick by using medicine, medical tools, or even astromy—went back and forth between patients, distributing medicine.

In the bed farthest away from the door, they found a patient covered in bandages. Bags of ice sat on his chest and arms, and a wet cloth lay on his forehead.

"Are these friends of Mr. Jones?" asked the nurse.

"That's Malcolm!" Alasha yelled.

Yenny said, "Oh, no."

Brian, however, was just stunned. He had thought Malcolm Jones was invincible, the type of guy he himself wanted to be. To see the great adventurer crippled in bed for trying to be a hero sent a pang through Brian's heart.

"It seems he tried to break into the mansion to rescue you," Professor Chaff explained solemnly. "He must have tried to sneak in through the basement, because that's where he was when Mamlith's astromy backfired and the building collapsed. The medicist said he should eventually make a substantial recovery, but it will be a long and difficult road."

"He tried to help us," Yenny said. Suddenly he ran outside, then came back with a bundle of unusual, star-shaped purple flowers Brian had never seen before. Brian assumed Yenny had grown them.

"We'll keep you all posted," the medicist said, ushering them outside.

With Mamlith finally out of the picture, Brian and Alasha were free to focus on other goals. They no longer feared they'd be harassed by the Red Robes.

Alasha used the money she had saved up by selling jewelry and bought Yenny new clothes at the market square. She tried to convince Yenny to let her buy him something nice, as she was sure the kid had never worn anything fancy before, but eventually they settled on what she thought was a pretty boring outfit: simple jeans and a plain brown shirt with a hood, which he put up whenever he was around people.

The more people there were in a group, the less likely Yenny was to talk. When speaking to more people than just Brian and Alasha, Yenny became intent on looking at his shoes and was prone to blushing when addressed. Alasha felt so bad for how nervous Yenny seemed around other people that she convinced Brian to take him into the Flaming Forest to practice wood astromy. Her plan worked; before they even reached the tree line, Yenny smiled ear to ear and walked with a hop in his step.

"It's too bad you came to town when so much bad was happening," said Alasha. "Do you like the cones?"

"They're great!" said Yenny merrily.

The first cones of the early evening began to ignite above them. First the brown cones crackled, then puffs of white smoke rose from the seeds, and finally came the red-orange light.

"Fireworks, no!" Alasha said. Nearby, Fireworks amused himself by trying to catch chuboroughs, spade-footed rodents who kept digging in and out of the earth, trying to gather fallen nuts and berries. Across the river, sunlight glimmered on the windows of the houses on the bay and yellowed the huge rocks that served as the bridge from one bank to the other.

"Do they hurt if you pick them up?" Yenny asking, inspecting a lit cone that had fallen to the ground at his feet.

"Only if you hold tightly," Alasha said, picking the red, crackling cone off the ground and placing it in Yenny's hands. It was warm, and occasionally gave a small *pop* as the cone seeds crackled. "Brian showed me this place a few years ago. So beautiful, the kind of place I want my love to take me to."

"Why don't you build Alasha a house out here?" Yenny asked,

glancing at Brian. "You're rich enough to."

"My sign is the Snow Swan," Alasha interjected. She was on her knees, trying to feed nuts to little critters. "Swans are independent and go after their goals themselves."

"What she's saying is, she's too proud," Brian butted in.

Alasha went on as though she hadn't heard him. "Snow Swans like the solitude and the quiet places, especially magical natural spots like this. Just need some snow, and it would be perfect. Oh, they're so cute!" One of the rodents rolled into her hands.

"You do believe me, don't you?" Yenny asked. "About me being the Day King?"

"Well," Alasha said, putting the animal back down, "it's just . . ."

Brian said, "A better question is, Yenny, why do *you* think you're the Day King?"

"Do you think anyone might come along?" Yenny asked. "I mean, are we alone here in the woods?"

"Yes, we're alone," Alasha said.

"Here's a trick I learned," Yenny said, pointing toward the clouds. "You see that really bright star in the north? It's Zenith, the Star of the King." Yenny waved his hand in an arc above his head.

Brian and Alasha both craned their necks to look up at Zenith. It could have been one of the fire cones, but it looked to Brian as if the light from Zenith flashed across the sky. Had Yenny done something to elicit that spark?

"Why didn't you do that earlier?" Alasha asked, looking from Zenith back to Yenny.

"My mentor told me not to," Yenny said. "He didn't want

people instantly knowing who I was, in case there was trouble."

"You can't trust everyone," Alasha agreed.

Brian still didn't know how he felt, sitting on the ground, crunching up leaves. If the stars really had chosen a new Day King, why would they have picked such a silly, wimpy kid?

From deeper in the woods, a shrill scream rang out. Brian, Yenny, and Alasha froze and exchanged glances.

Yenny asked, "Is it the Red Robes?"

"They're all gone," Alasha answered, looking deeper into woods. "They left when Mamlith died. Same with the malkins."

Another scream tore the air asunder, this one even louder.

Brian leapt to his feet. "I'll go check it out," he said. "You two go get help."

"Don't you think Fireworks and I should check it out?" Yenny said. "You should go get help."

"Excuse me," Alasha said. "I'm the oldest. You guys leave and get help."

"I'm the astromer here," Brian argued, "so I should go!"

"Yenny's done more astromizing than you," Alasha retorted.

"So I'll go!" Yenny cheered.

"No, you definitely stay here," Alasha said, placing a hand on his shoulder.

"I'm not staying here," Brian and Yenny said at the same time.

Rolling her eyes, Alasha said, "Fine! We'll all go, but stay behind me."

Alasha led the way through the trees in the direction of the screaming. They crept past the ember pine trees, stepping over fallen, smoldering pine cones.

"That's Malcolm's house," Alasha said.

It was a simple brick house that Malcolm had built himself. The corners of the house were already covered with cobwebs, and the chain-link fence surrounding the place was bent, probably by animals trying to get into the abandoned house to search for food. Brian could see a locked door in the grassy ground next to a cement wall, and a peg with a key and a long whistle was hanging a few feet above it.

"Did the screams come from here?" Yenny asked.

Before Brian could answer, several screams came from behind the locked door. Yenny grabbed the key and opened the door on the ground. They looked down and saw a set of cracked wooden stairs that led into darkness. From where they stood, constant shrieking could be heard.

"I think we should go get help," Alasha said.

"Someone's screaming down there!" Brian argued.

"They might need our help," Yenny said.

"If we're being honest, none of us can really fight," Alasha snapped.

Brian walked back to the woods and grabbed a fallen branch covered with glowing pine cones. When he returned, Yenny's eyes were wide and eager, but Alasha was pursing her lips.

"Better?" Brian asked. "Let's go."

Giving a long sigh, Alasha grabbed the whistle from its peg and clutched it tightly. "A whistle . . ." she muttered to herself. "But why?"

Brian led the group through the door, trying to be quiet. However, Yenny seemed not to understand the situation, and his feet fell heavily.

At the sound of their steps on the floor, the shrieking stopped. Brian walked down what felt like twenty steps until he reached a gravel floor, his feet sinking slightly in the small stones. He coughed as he breathed the hot, moist air; he was already sweating. It smelled like a zoo.

Someone touched Brian's elbow, and he jumped.

"It's me," Yenny said, his face barely visible by the light of the pine cones. Brian breathed more normally and looked around, trying to see into the darkness. He could now make out the twisting tunnels, which were lined with cages.

Someone shrieked nearby. Brian, Yenny, and Alasha jumped, alarmed—the scream hadn't come from behind, but above. Alasha took the branch from Brian, pointed the pine cones to the ceiling, and saw a terrible sight.

A large bat, about twice the size of a human, hung from the ceiling. It didn't appear to have eyes, but its head turned in their direction, its nostrils opening to smell the air. It shrieked again and flew down.

Alasha pushed Yenny aside, and the giant bat flew into the ground, spraying dirt and rocks everywhere. More shrieking came from behind them, and Brian saw dark shapes move in their direction.

Yenny screamed, but Alasha blew the whistle. A high-pitched sound ripped through the tunnel, hurting Brian's ears. The giant bats flew over them, flapping in circles. Alasha pulled Yenny to the side, and they crawled their way to the side of the room.

"They're camazots," Alasha whispered. "They're blind, but they respond to sound and movement. The whistle that was hanging up there can control them."

Brian, Yenny, and Alasha sat quietly on the ground. The camazots crawled on their wings in the dirt, shrieking and confused by the whistle. Their heads turned from side to side, trying to catch a noise.

Alasha tapped Brian and then Yenny, who seemed to be trying his hardest not to breathe. She pointed first to the whistle, then to the stairs they had come down. Brian hoped he understood her meaning: she wanted them to run after she blew the whistle.

"You want me to throw the whistle upstairs?" Yenny asked loudly.

Brian winced. The camazots jumped into the air at once and flew at Brian, Yenny, and Alasha. Brian and Alasha screamed, but Yenny waved his arm. A giant root broke through the ground and swatted the bats into the wall so hard Brian heard the wall crack. Alasha blew the whistle as hard as she could, and the camazots yelled loudly, flying around madly in the dark cellar. Brian grabbed Alasha's hand, Alasha grabbed Yenny's hand, and they ran to the stairs

They made it out and tried to close the door, but they were knocked backward as the camazots flew out of the cellar after them. On his back, Brian saw three of them fly into the sky. Two of them landed next to them.

Alasha grabbed a stick and jammed it into the nostril of the closest one. Brian pressed his hands to the ground, urging his astromy to finally manifest. Now was the time!

Yenny tried to catch the closest one with roots, but the bat flew out of reach. It then reached for Yenny with one of its clawed feet.

Fireworks ran past Yenny and breathed out a ball of crackling green fire. The fireball blew up right in the camazot's face. Blue fire quickly engulfed the closest one, which screamed and flew away. The remaining camazot was chased away by Fireworks, and they screeched angrily as they flew into the sky.

"Camazots," Alasha said, helping Yenny up. "In Malcolm's own house."

"What made the Red Robes decide to use camazots?" Yenny asked.

"Malcolm is good at talking to bats. I suppose they got the idea from him," Alasha said. "Come on, let's get out of here."

They ran back to Brian's house, all the whole looking upward and keeping an eye out for giant bats; but the skies were clear.

11

Astromy Lessons

Lord Elyon sat in semidarkness. It was late in the night, and a distant storm thundered outside the walls. He sat on his throne as though waiting for something. His staff, which bore a ram's head, was propped on the wall as he stroked a round orb, a stone as black as the Light Baetylus was white. Around him were several people in black robes. They were mapping the stars in the sky and writing notes about celestial movements, muttering their findings amongst themselves.

A figure walked through the open door, the clinking of metal armor filling the room. The person kept their distance just at the edge of the moonlight, so only the merest green glint shone in the shadows.

"Welcome, my old friend. Once again, I have need of your services," said Elyon.

The armored person did not bow or speak.

Lord Elyon continued: "I must say I am surprised. It's been a long time I've seen your weapons so clean. No work lately?" He paused, then continued when he was met with silence. "My Light Baetylus has been stolen in a town called Vennisburg, in the Ember Region of Kama. Your mission is very simple: retrieve it as quickly as possible. You see the Shadow Baetylus in my possession, but unless all ten Baetyli are ours, the plan will not proceed smoothly."

At last, the armor moved, turning back toward the door.

"My last word to you is this," Lord Elyon added. "There is no need to keep secret. Feel free to show off."

It was just after sunset, and a pink line was visible on the horizon. Hundreds of red-orange spots fell to ground in the Flaming Forest across the river.

Alasha had prepared another Touketian meal called *pelmini*, or ear bread. It was meat wrapped in a very thin dough. Brian thought Alasha's *pelmini* was always delicious. Professor Chaff was in one of the guest rooms, making notes.

"I bet if we had the Fire Baetylus, we could make the pine cones light up like the sun," Yenny said.

"Right, so tell me about these stone things again. How do they help with astromy?" Brian asked.

"They're the sources!" Yenny opened his bag. Brian and Alasha gazed upon the Light Baetylus. It was shimmering white.

"So, this giant pearl is the source of light itself. *All* the light on the planet comes from *this*," mocked Brian, plucking the round jewel from Yenny's hand. He let out a "Ha!" loud enough to awaken every critter in the surrounding forest.

"You don't believe me," moaned Yenny, looking at the table.

"No offense, Yenny, but there's no proof. It's a scam, like the Day Kings and Night Lords and all the other stuff. We wouldn't have kings or queens already if we had Day Kings."

"Day Kings have lived," said Alasha. "They in books. The last was one of the winged folk, like Yenny." She pointed her finger dangerously close to Yenny's purple eye. "What's not to believe?"

"Why would Day Kings have to be sent miraculously from someone?" asked Brian, shrugging and pushing his emptied bowl away. "Even Chaff says it's not true, and she knows everything. Right, Chaff?" Brian called to the room where she was making notes; but all they heard was Professor Chaff muttering to herself. "To me, if I can't touch it or see it, it might as well not exist. Why hide?"

"He has wings!" Alasha shouted. "Can't you see *that*?"

"That doesn't mean anything. Maybe he . . ." Brian went quiet, trying to think of a good explanation for Yenny's wings. "I just don't like the idea of people or stars telling me what I can and can't be. What if I wanted to be king? I couldn't do that because some star said so? That's the dumbest thing I ever heard."

"That's what Master Paleo told me," Yenny said quietly.

His eyes were becoming red, as if he was about to cry, so Brian thought for a change of topic. "So, what would you do if you had all the Baetyli, Yenny?"

"What do you mean?" asked Yenny.

"The Stones are the source of the forces of nature—at least, that's what you think. We could probably use them like supercharged fuels or something, or do astromy we could never do on our own. If I had the Lightning Baetylus, I'd bring down a bolt of lightning so I'd never have to go to school again. Teachers—"

"If I had the Ice Baetylus, I wouldn't need to go all the way home to see the snow. I'd put a pile of snow outside and play all day," Alasha said, her eyes momentarily closed as she imagined her winter wonderland. "What about you, Yenny?"

"I'd use it to find my family," Yenny answered. "Combining all ten together is supposed to make one all-powerful and all-knowing. You could use them to do whatever you wanted."

Alasha abruptly stopped smiling "What happened to them?" she asked.

"I don't know. But I think the Crazy Man does."

"Who's the Crazy Man?" Brian asked.

"He's the only thing I remember," Yenny said nonchalantly. "I don't know what happened to my family and friends. I heard they all scattered and went into hiding, but I don't have memories—except for the Crazy Man."

"What does he look like?" Brian asked.

"It's just a face. A red face that's . . . that's laughing at me. I dream about him sometimes."

"You don't just have someone's face in your memory without ever meeting them," said Brian.

"I think I know the person. But every time I come close to finding out, he runs away. But he always comes back to laugh at me again."

"You could've had a head attack," suggested Alasha. "I think that is what people call 'callingsin.'"

"A concussion," Brian corrected.

"That's why I'm looking for all ten Baetyli," Yenny continued. "Their power combined can make a wish reality. If I can just find them . . ." Yenny's eyes and voice dropped.

"How do you even know the stones could do all of this?" Brian asked. "My neighbor is the astromy expert, and she never told me the Baetyli could do those things."

"It's all thanks to Master Paleo. He's a saint, and he's the one all the Angeli and other leaders go to. Ancient events are his specialty, probably because he's old. But don't tell him that," Yenny added quickly, looking suddenly scared.

"Wait, Paleo?" Brian racked his memory. "The famous Paleo I always read about in the papers? Isn't he supposed to be some kind of phony?"

"No!" Yenny said, his voice echoing among the trees. "I mean . . . you heard wrong." He tried to say something more, but instead, just looked down at the table.

"I'm with Yenny," Alasha said. "Master Paleo the most famous saint alive, and he not made a mistake yet. So many people just jealous of him, that's all. Has he taken care of you?"

"For the past year," said Yenny proudly. "Before I met him, I lived in Bosque Forest with the mystics."

"You've lived with *mystics*?" Alasha asked. The nature mystics, also known as the elves, made their homes in star terrain, land that had its own natural astromy. "They hardly show themselves to anyone. They not human?"

"They're definitely human, just a little different," Yenny said. "They're so mysterious than a lot of people think they aren't human at all, so they call them elves. I've actually never seen them fully before. They are always cloaked and never stayed to talk to me. They just sent me food and told the animals to look after me. All they said was that I was important. That's when Paleo showed up. He and the other mystics told me who I was and that I was meant to be king. They knew that the whole time and never told me."

"So Paleo asked you to join him?" Alasha asked excitedly.

"Well, he didn't really ask," Yenny admitted. "He sort of just dragged me along. He wanted to teach me how to be a wise king, but he said I couldn't do that unless I saw the world. So we've been traveling together this whole time, and he's been teaching me everything about the stars and what each constellation means . . . ."

The next thing Brian knew, cold water splashed across his head. He got up soaking wet, half expecting to be attacked.

"What was that for?" Brian asked.

"You keep falling asleep on him," Alasha said.

"He used to live with elves," Brian cried. "I heard him! But I still want to know what makes Paleo so special. Even Professor Chaff is a big fan of him, and she needs equations and theories before she'll believe anything."

Brian grabbed a napkin and pressed it against his wet face while Yenny continued: "Saints and wizards are astromers whose connection to the stars is so strong that they can actually see the future and tell us what the stars want us to do. Saints are people who use this for good, and wizards use this power for bad. Master Paleo told me the future can be read in the stars and how they move with the planets. That's Paleo's job as a saint. Kings and queens always beg him for advice before making big decisions." Yenny yawned loudly and rubbed his eyes.

"Where have you been sleeping?" Alasha asked.

"At random motels," Yenny answered. "It's kind of lonely. I don't have any friends besides you two."

"Aww," Alasha said.

"Huh," Brian said. He felt a twinge in his temple as he struggled to ask the question. "Did you *want* to stay here?"

Yenny's purple eyes opened wider than Brian he had ever seen them. "Yes! You mean it? But I don't have any money."

"Don't worry about it. You deserve some peace and quiet," was Brian's reply, and he avoided looking Yenny in the eye. "But keep it quiet. I'm meeting Professor Chaff tomorrow morning to talk astromy."

"Can I come?" Yenny asked.

"I don't care," Brian said. "Do what you want." He walked to the stairway. "Hey, Chaff, we're calling it a night. Are we still good for tomorrow?"

"For your astromy lesson?" came her voice, and Brian could just make out the top of her bushy head near the front door. "Of course. Always happy to impart knowledge. Yenny and Alasha should come." She walked out and closed the door behind her.

"I have a buyer for some Touketian earrings I need to finish," Alasha said.

"I want to go," Yenny said. Brian shrugged.

"Where will you be sleeping, by the way?" Brian asked. But he wasn't really listening; a group of cute girls had walked into the view from his front window, giggling as they walked down the sidewalk in the twilight.

"Uh, right here seems good enough," Yenny said, pointing to the couch in the family room.

But the girls outside had stopped to pull pine cone cinders out of each other's hair. Brian raised his voice unnecessarily. "Sleep wherever you want, Yenny. Because my house has enough room for YENNY THE KRYSTEE to stay tonight! He's a hero, so I'd love for him to stay *here* . . . in my *house!*"

But the girls were so deep in conversation, they apparently did not hear a thing. Brian waited another minute, then walked upstairs. Yenny had already pulled a very thick blanket out of his bag. It appeared to be made of soft white feathers.

"Ooh, that looks beautiful," said Alasha as she entered the room in her nightgown.

"It's the only thing I have from my mother," Yenny explained. "She said the feathers are made from the wings of my guardian angel. When I sleep with it over me, he protects me."

"That was nice to say," said Alasha, the moonlight reflecting off her light blue eyes. "I know you will meet the angel soon."

"Yeah, he might even be in town tomorrow morning," Brian joked from the corner of the room.

"Do either of you have brothers or sisters?" Yenny asked as he curled up on the couch.

"No, we're both only kids," Brian said.

"Did you want a younger brother or sister?" Yenny asked. Yenny's tone sounded as though he was begging.

"I wish I did," Alasha sighed while tying her hair up. "Someone I could look after, teach how to cook, hug goodnight—"

"Could you do that?" Yenny interrupted.

Brian and Alasha stared dumbly at him.

Yenny flushed. "I mean, you know, the last part."

"Hug you goodnight?" Alasha asked.

"I mean, if you want to," Yenny said. His face could have cooked an egg, and Brian could have thrown up.

"Yes!" Alasha ran over and wrapped her arms around Yenny before walking away as though she had saved the world.

"That was the first time anyone hugged me!" Yenny whispered to Brian, smiling. "It felt great." Brian couldn't speak. Instead, he watched Yenny turn on his side and fall asleep.

"I can't stand foxes," Brian muttered. Suddenly bored, he walked to his own bedroom and fell asleep at once. His last thoughts were about what kinds of things Professor Chaff might teach him the next day.

"Brian! Wake up already!"

Brian woke immediately, partly out of fear of being roused with cold water again. After getting up and finding some clothes to wear, Brian left the room and met the scent of his favorite breakfast.

"Professor Chaff made breakfast today," Alasha said from the couch, where she was fastening chanstones into a silver bracelet. "She wanted you to have your favorite before your lesson."

"Yes, blueberry breakfast cakes!" Brian cheered. "Do you still have that Touketian honey with you?"

Brian spent his first fifteen minutes of the day eating breakfast cakes sweetened with honey, washing it down with hippoverd milk. "Where the heck is the Manda-dumb, anyway?" he asked, peering around for Yenny's oversized ears.

"He's out at the lake. And it's 'Mandalah', not what you just said. And be nice."

"Nope. I'll see you at some point," said Brian as he opened the door.

But he stopped. A nasty smell had just reached his nose. "Alasha, do you smell anything?" He looked at Alasha and was surprised to see her giggling.

"Yenny said that the kitsune thought he was staying a while and Fireworks . . . well, you know . . . marked his space." Alasha suppressed the onslaught of giggles and went to making her necklace.

Brian whispered, "Marked his space," knowing full well what Alasha meant. "I'm going to tie its tails in a double knot," Brian replied through gritted teeth. He shut the door harder than he had anticipated and walked to the fence.

Next door, Professor Chaff was exiting her house, wearing

her usual white lab coat over her suit and tie, her black briefcase in her right hand so her left wrist would be free for a silver watch. In her chest pocket was a small spiral notebook and pens in case she ever wanted to make up a new equation on the spot.

"Morning, Brian. How's the young hero of the village doing?"

"Still a little sleepy," Brian replied.

"You're about to get free education and you're sleepy. When I was your age, I jumped for joy whenever teachers wanted to teach me something."

"What? The only thing I learned from you is that math is boring."

"Math is boring?" Professor Chaff said, offended. "My young man, let me explain the wonders of math to you. Without math, you wouldn't be able to—"

But Brian had already checked out. He just let her talk as they went all the way to the lake. They were interrupted only twice, by groups of neighbors congratulating Brian about the victory at Mamlith's.

They continued up the road to the outskirts of town, where there were fewer people. Upon crossing the wooden fence that separated the main road from the lake's banks, they discovered Yenny playing fetch with Fireworks.

"Okay, you're both here," said Professor Chaff, looking from Yenny to Brian. "Let's start with the basics. Brian, I believe you still struggle with the basics of what astromy is."

"I know what the basics are," Brian protested. "All you do is force your energy into different materials and make them do whatever."

The professor scoffed. To her, anything less than a textbook answer was blasphemy. "I have told you several times already. In its most basic definition, astromy is the act of flowing energy into or alongside any of the ten forces of nature, for the purpose of work and recreation. Do you know what the forces of nature are, Yenny?"

"Fire, wind, ice, water, wood, earth, lightning, light, darkness, and death," Yenny recited.

"That's correct: pretty much everything except time itself. And which one have we not been successful with?"

"Death," Yenny answered.

"Correct!" the professor answered. "Death remains the only force that has yet to be properly astromized; it still remains a purely academic theory. It has long been theorized that stars are the source of astromy; whether the Stones of Life influence astromy has not yet been proven. But as you have probably heard, the Astromy Age is nearing its end; there aren't nearly as many astromers left.

"The term *astromy* gained popularity in the early nineteenth century. Astrogists like myself thought it was more scientifically accurate, and relieved religious tensions among those who considered astromy occult. General feats of astromy performed by humans are still sometimes called miracles; likewise, astromy used for evil is often considered witchcraft."

"Can you explain how astromy works when it doesn't come from people?" Yenny asked excitedly, while Brian couldn't care less. "Like the Flaming Forest?"

"It's not just humans that benefit from the stars," the professor said, smiling even bigger than Yenny, as she often did when she found an engaging student. "Many natural landscapes have inherited power from the stars and exhibit powerful qualities, to which we add the 'star' prefix. The Flaming Forest, for example, has pine cones that ignite in accordance with the moons' cycle. Those are called *star trees*. The continent Miazu is famous for its star water and its three star mountains, which are all also magical. Magic, by the way, is what we call the astromy that is found naturally in animals or even places, such as Zapharista Castle in Nydist City, without humans doing anything. Magic is usually unstable and formless, but its power is a part of nature itself. These are the lands where you would find the mystics."

"So, basically, if I live in these magic places, I can become more powerful?" Brian asked. If the answer was yes, he'd have five-story house with a large pool built in the Flaming Forest in a week.

"Dwelling in a magical environment safely can only be done through the practices of the people who live there. Exposure to natural astromy in the absence of proper handling can lead to diffuse apoptosis and protein splicing, and can rearrange the pathways in your limbic system and prefrontal cortex."

"Did you understand any of those words?" Brian asked Yenny, who shook his head.

"You turn into a malkin," the professor said.

"What!" the boys exclaimed.

"Yes indeed, although we can't yet scientifically map out the entire process. The human body can't handle but so much power at once; it'll destroy your body and devolve you. The earliest malkins were ancient tribes who tried to use magic to turn themselves into astromers who could control the forces of nature on a greater scale. Again, you'll hear many talks about witchcraft and possession being the reason behind malkins' existence."

Having finished her astromy review, Professor Chaff continued by saying, "Brian, one of your main problems is that you don't gather enough energy. Without the appropriate amount of power, the object you attempt to astromize will not respond to you. In moderate cases, your target might move in a direction you don't intend, potentially causing injury to you. In severe cases, the object might absorb too much astromy and blow up."

"Okay, so how can I get better?" asked Brian, rubbing his eyes. Professor Chaff's voice must have been magical too; it always made Brian sleepy.

"All astromy runs on a time limit, starting at around five seconds," the professor explained, walking a short distance in the ankle-high grass through which grasshoppers could be seen jumping around. "You're a beginner, so the energy you have to put into earth runs out quickly. I am willing to bet that you can break the earth and raise it, but still haven't reached levitation yet—a big milestone many young earth astromers can't wait for." She stopped and poked a large rock nearby. "This rock is twenty pounds. At your current level, you should be able to move this forward about fifty-seven feet before it goes outside your range, but you will only have about ten seconds' worth of energy."

"How come I never had to worry about a time limit?" Yenny asked.

"Because all krystees are naturally born with the ability to perform astromy. You don't have to worry about time limits or touching the elements; you can do it with your mind! Go ahead."

Yenny chose a spot and focused closely on it. A small tree slowly grew out of the ground. Yenny held both of his hands forward, squeezed really hard, and gritted his teeth, and the tree grew even faster, as if time had accelerated. Leaves unfolded, and branches started zigzagging in all directions. Brian gnashed his teeth in jealousy.

"Anyone who is not a krystee would have to touch a living tree to do that, and would be unable to grow trees that couldn't survive in this location. What everyone who is not a krystee performs is really an imitation that your own people taught us.

"Now it's Brian's turn!" the professor said excitedly.

Brian touched the earth and forced as much energy as he could into it. Cracks started to appear. The professor pulled Brian away immediately and said, "Not too much at once. You'll break it and send chunks of rock everywhere. Imagine yourself inflating a balloon. Fill the inside, starting from the center outward. If you're naturally an earth type, then your energy will automatically take on earth qualities without you having to do anything."

Brian placed his hands on the rock once again and strained his mind, imagining the rock like a balloon. The large rock immediately slid forward with more ease than Brian had ever experienced. Eventually it slowed down, then stopped completely.

Professor Chaff jogged from the spot where the boulder had started moving to where it had finished. She hunched over and traced the marks in the dirt with her fingers.

"Yep, fifty-seven feet. Actually, that's more about sixty feet and two and a half inches, so good for you," Professor Chaff praised.

"You can tell all that just by looking?" Yenny asked, impressed.

"I have been working with measurements longer than you've been alive," the Professor said with pride. "That's how you push, Brian. To attract is a little different and slightly harder. It's like turning yourself into a magnet. You continuously coat your hands with a layer of your own energy; the more force to you want to come to you, the thicker the layer has to be. This has the dual purpose of attracting a force to your flesh and protecting your body from harmful forces such as fire, lightning, or poisonous plants. It might even protect you from killing yourself when performing death astromy."

Brian put his arm forward and imagined a glove of energy around it. His imagination might have done it, but he thought he could *see* the air around his hand wave slightly—even glow, a dull blue-purple.

"Now touch the ground and send your energy through the ground to the rock. Astromy only works through skin-to-surface contact. Send it to the rock and you will be able to move it, although the farther an object is from you, the harder it is to levitate. You'll have an easier time of this since earth isn't fluid."

"I got this." Brian touched the ground and tried to move the same rock. It slowly floated back to him, though not so linearly or smoothly. Brian's happiness went away when the rock kept coming. He stepped aside before breaking into a run, but the rock kept chasing him.

"Stop using your energy. It's developed an attraction to you," the professor yelled. "This phenomenon is called *inanima caninact*, or 'inanimate dog,' if you wanted to know." Yenny just stood there and watched as Brian waved his hands wildly around as if he were trying to get something off of him. Eventually the large rock stopped, and Brian relaxed.

The professor clapped, hopping on the balls of her feet. "You see? Ah, physics is beautiful," said the professor with watery eyes.

"That was so easy," Brian said. "I'm ready to try other forces now. Yenny, bring out the Light Baetylus. I want to try astromizing light."

"The Light Baetylus?" the professor repeated incredulously.

"That's not here in town."

"Yes, it is. Don't you still have it, Yenny?"

"Of course I do. Fetch it, Fireworks."

"I'll believe it when I see it," Chaff responded.

Fireworks ran toward a nearby tree and grabbed the strap of Yenny's bag from the ground. He then ran back to Yenny and dropped the bag, from which Yenny pulled out the Light Baetylus.

Professor Chaff's mouth was as wide as the lenses of her glasses. "Impossible," she said. "Did Mamlith have this the whole time? This explains everything!" She pulled out a chisel with her left hand and a hammer with her right. "Let's break it open."

"No!" Yenny said, stepping back and covering the white stone defensively.

"It's not up to you, boy. That's an ancient artifact that has been sought for millennia."

"So you're going to *break* it?" Yenny hollered.

"It holds mysteries that astrogists like myself have made it our business to solve."

"But I still need it!" Yenny said, running behind the rock that Brian was practicing on.

"Brian, you go that way. I'll go this way," Professor Chaff said madly as she chased Yenny, apparently not noticing she was still holding the hammer. Brian didn't do anything, for he was too busy enjoying the show. Fireworks had started barking again, which Brian assumed was due to Professor Chaff chasing Yenny.

"Someone's—where?" Yenny asked, for only he had any hope of interpreting what Fireworks was saying. Still, listening more closely, Brian indeed recognized the pattern of the kitsune's barks. This was the same bark sequence he had made when they were attacked in the forest by the malkins. Which meant—

"What's going on?" Brian looked around, but there was no one to be seen.

"Fireworks said there's an invisible person in armor nearby. Right there!"

"Where?" Brian and Professor Chaff asked.

"Right there! Don't you see him?" Yenny pointed at a spot on the road.

Like a mirage, the silhouette of a man slowly came into view. He was covered head to foot in dark green armor.

12

Enter the Raider

Yenny tried to get a good look at the man, but there was no exposed skin to see. The man wore a mask that resembled a lion's face and matched the green hue of his armor, which covered his chest, arms, legs, back, and feet. What could have been mistaken for dreadlocks were actually ropes attached to his mask, in imitation of a lion's mane. Over his biceps and rib cage was black chainmail. Strange mechanisms and springs were fixed around his ankles and ran up his thighs. He raised his arm forward quickly.

A quick flash of metal flew out from the armored man, and Yenny felt a prick in his leg. The professor and Brian both fell to the ground.

"What did you do?" Yenny yelled. He knelt down quickly. They seemed to be drifting to sleep,

"How you're doing? Did I tell you I'm rich?" Brian's drooling mouth mumbled as his eyes closed.

"Arthroculus venom. Fascinating," said the professor before closing her eyes. Rachel Chaff was truly a scientist. Still, this meant Yenny was left on his own.

"Leave us alone, and you can have all my snacks," Yenny bargained. Maybe the man wouldn't hurt them if Yenny was pleasant to him.

The man unsheathed a blade. Yenny had the feeling that maybe he wasn't a snacking type of guy.

Fireworks barked a command.

"I can't leave these two," Yenny protested.

But Fireworks barked again, more urgently this time.

"I'm counting on you." Yenny did as he'd been told and grabbed the Stone. If Fireworks was right, the armored man would chase Yenny down.

Yenny held the Stone closer and ran, but did not go far before he stumbled, barely missing a barrage of darts the armored man had thrown. He got up and jumped the fence in one leap, making a straight a line to the Flaming Forest.

Yenny's mind was running faster than his legs. He had never really fought anyone before, and he did not want to test his beginner's luck now. What he wanted to know instead was what the hunter was prepared to do for the Baetylus.

He got his answer in the form of a metal palm. The armored man had outrun Yenny and hidden in the forest, and now his hand was in Yenny's face. How had he moved so quickly?

SLAP!

The world blinked out of focus, and Yenny fell against a tree, causing fire cones to cascade down and combust.

An idea ignited in Yenny's head. He glanced at a nearby branch filled with fire cones, and astromized it to swing like a whip at the hunter. A dozen flaming cones became bombs that hurtled down and combusted on impact into blinding red flames. A whirl of burning spices filled Yenny's nostrils, making him cough.

Yenny opened his watery eyes, and there the man was, less than a foot away. In one swift movement, metal hands closed around Yenny's neck, and he was lifted off the ground. He struggled and kicked, but the muscle behind the armor was strong. A white light flashed, and Yenny saw the Light Baetylus in the man's hand.

"I need that. I need all of them," Yenny sputtered, trying to summon the energy to astromize, but soon he was struggling just to breathe. A large stone pillar broke through the earth underneath them, and the man vanished before Yenny had hit the ground.

A familiar-looking boy stumbled into the clearing.

"Brian, what are you doing here?" Yenny asked surprised. He hadn't thought it was possible for Brian to wake from a dream about girls.

"The stupid fox thing." Brian winced. Fireworks had indeed gone a little overboard; there were teeth marks on Brian's arms, hands, legs, neck, and face. "Wait until I get my hands on that little—"

"But I thought you were asleep," Yenny said.

"Didn't Alasha say kitsune bites heal poison or something? That day we first met? Ouch! But you better be thankful I came back or you'd—"

Red needles fell between them as the trees rustled above, and Brian and Yenny fell into silence. Looking up together, they saw the armored man sitting among the branches; the lion's face, while stiff and metal, still leered hungrily, hiding in red needles.

The man jumped down, knives poised and ready to plunge. Brian and Yenny screamed, but the next instant, something remarkable silenced them.

Light, brighter than the light of the pine cone, broke through the trees. The light bore down on them like a heavy weight, sagging the boys' knees. The energy of it threw the armored attacker across the ground before crashing him into a tree. The man's body slumped at odd angles; he'd been knocked unconscious.

Yenny squinted and could just barely make out the form of a newcomer within the bright light. Whoever this man was, he was riding some sort of animal and waving a staff in the air. He wore no heavy chainmail, but instead seemed buried in robes. Yenny could not see the man's face, but whoever it was, the armored man hesitated to attack him. A showdown seemed imminent—but before Yenny or Brian could react, the armored man disappeared from the tree, vanishing as instantly as he'd appeared.

"He got scared?" Brian asked. Then a grin spread across his face. "He's a saint."

"Master Paleo!" Yenny called, causing the new arrival to turn around.

By saint standards, Master Paleo was not incredibly old—perhaps in his fifties, with gentle wrinkles on his face and hands. Master Paleo opened his mouth, and Yenny hoped to hear what the wise old saint would say about a dangerous situation.

"Well, don't you two both look pathetic," Master Paleo said. "How did he manage to beat up both of you?"

"That was a crazy guy in armor. I'm just a kid!" Brian said.

"So? I'm an older man, and I didn't have any problems. No excuses," the old master said.

"But," Brian said, "shouldn't you say something like 'Thou shalt not fight' or some fancy proverb?"

"Yeah, yeah," Master Paleo muttered as he turned to face Yenny. "Yenitus, all I asked you to do was find some milk for us, and you took days?" Paleo said. "I was reading the stars, and they pointed out that you might be in trouble."

The saint had flown in on a beast large enough for three people to ride. It looked like a large lion with a bull's horn sticking out of its head, with wings the same color as its golden-brown fur.

"A *lamassu?*" Brian said. "Why are you riding a lamassu?"

Yenny understood Brian's confusion. Lamassus were often untamable and flew dangerously high, so people preferred riding quellows, large birds with little gardens and sometimes even trees on their backs.

"Supersonic Airmaster is the best steed ever," Yenny said. As he said its name, the creature noticed Yenny for the first time. It lowered its owllike head into a bow.

"Supersonic Airmaster?" Brian said, still gaping at the lamassu. "You choose the worst names, Yenny."

"Excuse me. *I* named him Supersonic Airmaster," Master Paleo said proudly. "I think it's a pretty cool name, if you ask me."

"Oh," Brian said lamely. "I mean, cool name. Really cool name."

"Yenny, I think we should be leaving," Master Paleo said tersely. "We're only a day's flight away."

"Do we . . . do we have to fly?" Yenny asked nervously.

"Fine, we'll fly low and take it easy," Master Paleo promised, shaking his head. "One of these days we're going to toughen you up."

"So that's it?" Brian said. "You're just leaving?" He hadn't expected to feel weird seeing Yenny leave, as if he'd miss the krystee.

"I have to find the other Baetyli, remember?" The lamassu knelt so that Yenny could more easily grab onto its owl feathers and dog fur. I'll come back to visit," Yenny said from atop the lamassu. He waved at Brian.

"Go as fast as you can! None of your snail's pace this time," said Master Paleo.

"But you said . . ." Yenny started—but the lamassu ran down the lane, which led out of Vennisburg. The creature flapped its great wings and soared up above the ground. With each flap of its wings, it carried Paleo and Yenny higher. Paleo *woohoo*ed and Yenny *boohoo*ed, both at the top of their lungs.

"Good luck!" Brian shouted at last as Yenny, Master Paleo, and the lamassu took off into the sky.

"Brian! What in the name of Theo happened to you two?" asked Alasha as Brian and the professor barged into the clinic, covered in dirt, with a bruise visible on Brian's cheek. Professor Chaff had wanted Brian to stop by to get checked after being attacked.

Alasha came charging in right to Brian. "Why didn't you say you were attacked? You've got blood on face, and teeth are wobbly . . . ."

"Alasha, that's not blood. It's dirt. We were only attacked by a madman. Happens all the time now," said Brian. He then noticed whose bed Alasha was standing next to.

Malcolm Jones was still wrapped head to foot in bandages. Brian wondered if the man was awake, until Malcolm turned his head slightly in Brian's direction and squeezed his fists.

"So, what happened?" Alasha asked.

Since Professor Chaff had been knocked out for most of the event, Brian did most of the explaining about the armored man, the ensuing fight, and Yenny's flight with Master Paleo. Alasha listened to their story, and didn't speak until Brian stopped.

"So he didn't want Yenny," Alasha summed up, "but the Light Baetylus. But what was the man's name?"

"I don't know *who* he was, but I know *what* he was," said Professor Chaff.

"What is he?" she asked.

"Judging from his armor and his silence, I can only conclude that he must be part of a group of skilled bounty hunters called the Raiders," answered Chaff.

"What are they?" Alasha asked.

"They can be anything. Thieves, soldiers, living legends—as long as they are paid the right amount. They were used quite often until about two hundred years ago," she answered.

"What changed two hundred years ago?" Alasha asked.

"The Raiders were deemed too untrustworthy. The people who hired them were often betrayed when an enemy offered a higher payout. It would appear a small number of them continue to thrive in secret, probably working for crime bosses and rich gangs. The skills they possess are supposed to be legendary."

"Do they all have the same stuff?" asked Alasha. She gestured to her arms and chest, so it was clear she meant "armor," a word she had not been taught in her native tongue and often forgot.

"They all wear armor, yes," the professor responded, "but the designs vary according to their specialties. Some of the killer types wear different styles, but the one today was dressed for theft and secrecy. History books state that they were experimented on to heighten their abilities, but in the process, they were mutilated so horrifically that they wear armor and masks out of shame for their bodies." She walked to the window and peeped from behind a curtain.

"So I survived a fight with a world-class fighter who can take down a dozen warriors?" Brian asked. "Man, I'm good!"

"If you had been the main target, you wouldn't have survived," Chaff said solemnly. "He wanted the Baetylus. I conclude he was likely sent by someone who has strong ties to Mamlith. Someone must know that Mamlith is no longer in power."

They all sat quietly for a moment, except for Malcolm, who had started a fresh wave of angry groaning and thrashing that could only have been caused from agonizing pain. The nurse came forward and tried to feed him medicine, but he refused, until Chaff helped to force him down onto the bed.

"Like I was saying," said Professor Chaff, "the armored man won't be coming back here again. There's a high probability that he'll go where the other Baetyli are located, since that's what Yenny is looking for. Listen, it's late and I have five books to write. It's times like these I really wish I *could* astromize time. Let's go home. All three of us are done for the night."

"We have stuff to do," Brian argued.

"I'll fix us all some food," the professor offered.

At the word "food," Brian and Alasha headed toward the door, ready to go home.

"Yenny, you can open your eyes now."

"Fireworks says we're still high in the air," Yenny said. As different as Yenny and Fireworks were, they had one thing in common: they were both scared of heights.

Master Paleo brought Supersonic Airmaster so close to the ground, Yenny thought he could hear the creature's feet scrape the grass. Yenny opened his eyes slowly and looked around. The sunlight between the hills was blinding. To their right, a pack of regalants were hunting, their deer legs propelling them with haste while their lion's faces snapped and snarled. Yenny could tell which ones were male because they had antlers on their heads.

"Master Paleo, may I ask a question?" Yenny asked. Fireworks sat between Yenny's arms, waving both tails below Yenny's chin.

"Ask away," replied Paleo.

"You said we're going to Shiroho City. I know it's the capital of Kama, but what's there for us?"

"Shiroho is the home of the current Angelus, Christopher Cindoran. He is the only one who knows the exact location of the Fire Baetylus."

"What about the others?"

"Each of the seven Angeli is entrusted with the whereabouts of a Baetylus. The Fire Baetylus is located here in Kama. But the other Stones are located elsewhere."

"Do you know where?" Yenny probed.

"It is not my place to—"

"Please?" Yenny whined. "If you tell me, I'll be quiet. I know you hate when I ask questions."

"I really do," Master Paleo muttered. "Well, in that case: Each Baetylus is located in the continent to which its natural force corresponds. For example, the Fire Baetylus is located in Kama. The Shadow Baetylus and the Death Baetylus are lost in Mictland. And you have the Light Baetylus."

"So why don't we go to Mictland and search there first?"

"Nonsense, boy. The Lost Continent belongs to the lost. Even malkins stay far away from there."

"What's there?"

"Nothing you will ever see." Master Paleo's tone was stern. Yenny knew the conversation was over.

"But we know where most of the Baetyli are, right?" said Yenny. "Alright! Let's go to Shiroho City first!"

"Not quite yet. We must take a quick detour. We'll head to Kacella and visit a very special place to pick up something that might prove useful to you . . . very useful to you indeed."

"What is it? Sweets?" Then Yenny remembered what Mamlith had said. "No. It's the weapon I'm supposed to have, isn't it?"

"Some people call it a weapon," Master Paleo admitted. "And it has been used as such. But it has much more useful purposes. Very useful to you indeed."

13

Good-bye, Vennisburg

The Raider's entrance into Vennisburg did not gain much attention. The village was still recovering from the perpetual state of fear they suffered under Mamlith's command, and Professor Chaff did not want to worsen that fear by announcing that a live Raider had casually come to town looking for a powerful artifact.

"Let's just forget about it for now. The Ember region guardians will take care of it," the professor told Brian. Alasha was already asleep on the couch.

"Why do we even have guardians?" asked Brian. "I thought the Angeli were in charge."

"Well," said Professor Chaff, taking a deep breath. "First, you must understand that Angeli, the collective term for the Great Lords and Ladies in power, were created around 354 AD by the krystees to compensate for the absence of the Day King. While Day Kings are powerful enough to rule the whole world on their own, no one else was destined to do so by the stars. So, for each of the seven continents—"

"There are eight continents, though," Brian corrected.

"Yes, but Mictland is uninhabited by humans. Too dangerous, and too much dark magic. Anyway, the position of Lord was created and given to the most powerful astromer on each continent."

"It's that easy?" asked Brian.

"Oh, there's much more to it than that; there are criminal background checks and physical examinations. Candidates must also take a test to see how well they know their continent's geography, history, people, and problems. At the end of this exam, the applicants write an essay about a fabricated problem and how to solve it. Formerly, Lord or Lady hopefuls had to astromize in just their undergarments, in case they possessed astromy-enhancing items. But recently, with astromy becoming a rarer feat with each successive decade, that last bit was finally dropped."

"Oh, that's more of what I was expecting," said Brian even more slowly. "So where did the governors come from?"

"In time, the Angeli had their hands full and proved unable to watch over large land masses. So each continent was systematically divided into smaller regions, each one ruled by a governor, who is usually one of the most intelligent guardians in an Angelus' employ. Vennisburg is in the Ember region, which is under the control of Governor Limber. As to where Mamlith came from, I have no idea. That's something I should have asked Limber himself."

But that was all Brian heard; he was already asleep. He gave a snore that was in sync with Alasha's. Professor Chaff looked back to see Brian asleep, his hand close to Alasha's. The professor gritted her teeth angrily before blowing out the candle and going to bed. Professor Chaff knew Yenny wouldn't have gone to sleep while she was discussing interesting things.

"We just passed into the land of Kacella," exclaimed Master Paleo as they soared over an ocean shore. "Lady Aviadine is the Queen of Kacella and head of the Angeli Council. She and I go way back to when we were teenagers."

"That's nice," whispered Yenny, who then closed his eyes and fell asleep.

Master Paleo used this opportunity to sneak higher into the sky. The Big Moon was missing only a thin sliver, and gave off bluish-white light, adding to the wonder of the cold but breathtaking experience of flying on a lamassu through the clouds.

"Brian! Alasha! Wake up!" Professor Chaff's voice was urgent.

Even from behind closed eyelids, Brian could see fire burning in the distance. He opened his eyes in a panic, looked at the window, and witnessed mighty flames searing the sky through the curtain.

Mamlith's forces had returned. Brian didn't want to believe it, but it was the only explanation that made sense; he could feel the heat from the couch he was sleeping on. He threw the curtain aside to look for the enemy.

"You were yelling for this?" demanded Brian. Alasha rushed to look out the window and gasped.

Professor Chaff's called from the next room, "If you thought I was going to let you miss this outstanding phenomenon of science and atmospheric wonder . . ."

"Flame blankets?" Alasha asked excitedly. "I haven't seen flame blankets yet!"

The three walked outside. Other villagers had gathered on the street. The entire eastern sky was covered in wavy sheets of blue, yellow, and orange. While it was not uncomfortable, Brian could feel the heat tickle him from where he stood. It made him sleepy. The street had turned a dark reddish-brown from the light above.

"Fire blankets!" Professor Chaff said. "The morning sunlight hits the *ares* clouds in the sky, and then they ignite. The higher clouds burn the hottest—those blue ones, see?"

"How come Touket doesn't have these?" Alasha asked with jealousy.

"Ares clouds wouldn't accumulate over Touket," Professor Chaff answered. "Ares cloud only form from star water that has evaporated."

They stood and watched the clouds burn like giant balls of cotton on fire for the next several minutes, until they extinguished like candles, leaving the sky a bright morning blue.

"Well, I have lectures to plan," said Professor Chaff, going back inside.

"I have jewelry to make," Alasha added, following her.

Brian stood there for a moment before deciding to get another free meal from the Flaming Café. On the way, he passed several people, and was surprised when they didn't show him the attention they had given him the day after he had defeated Mamlith. No one offered to shake his hand or give him a hug, but instead merely smiled as they walked past.

The Flaming Café was a small coffee shop filled with big puffy couches and dim, low lights. In the gift shop, people could buy magical crafts and sculptures, made from the wood of the Flaming Forests, that glowed at the same times as the trees they came from.

"Can I have my free meal, please?" Brian asked as soon as he walked through the door.

"Sorry, honey. I promised you a week's worth. Time to start

paying again," said Sarah, the manager, from behind the register.

Brian bought a cup of hot chocolate, sat at the counter blowing on it until it had cooled, gulped it down in two swigs, and walked briskly out of the café. He walked all the way back home, where he crashed onto the couch in the living room.

Five minutes later, Alasha came in, and Brian thought he caught the jingle of metal rings in her bag. She was about to start working on her new collection of Touketian earrings.

Brian had always known this would happen to him eventually. It had only been a week, and his status as a hero had already diminished, especially since Yenny's departure. Brian forced himself to admit to himself that the kid had done most of the work against Mamlith. Now that Yenny was gone, the handshakes, free meals, and pointing were no longer to be expected. Brian had been reduced to being the rich kid with a powerful astromer for a father.

Yenny, on the other hand, was with a renowned saint, traveling to awesome cities and looking for Stones that would make him even more powerful. "*I need this Stone. I need all of them.*" That was what he had said to the Raider.

Brian hopped off the bed and ran downstairs, where he found Alasha carefully tying blue thread into a snowflake pattern on a large ring.

"I finished making my new jewel," Alasha said, dropping the stuff in her hands and picking up the earrings. "They made from metal found in Touket only, so they have a unique sound." Alasha waved them, and they made a sound similar to that of a wind chime.

"That's nice," Brian said. "Where do you think Yenny is now?"

"Off to the capital," Alasha answered. "That's what he said."

"Shiroho City?" Brian asked. "When did he say that?"

"He didn't, but he wanted the Stones of Life, and Papa always says the Stones be held at the capital cities."

"That's common knowledge? How come I didn't know that?—Never mind. If that's common knowledge, wouldn't Raiders know that, too?"

"Yeah?" Alasha said. "I don't get what you're saying."

"Listen. The Raider knows Yenny is chasing those magic rocks. He knows where the nearest one of them is." And that was when Alasha jumped off the couch in shock.

"He'll go to Shiroho City to get Yenny!" she shouted, stumbling over the "R" in the capital's name.

"Yes."

"He'll do bad things to him. Cut his hands off, beat him with sticks, set him on fire!"

"Um . . . maybe?"

But Alasha's imagination was already running wild. "We have to tell Professor Chaff. Let's split up. I'll check her house," she said at last.

"I'll check her other home," said Brian. They both knew he meant the library.

He and Alasha parted ways, and Brian walked the few blocks to the library quickly.

A gem of the small town of Vennisburg, the library was a regional wonder, and probably the only reason Professor Chaff stuck around. Brian found her sitting at a desk that had more books on it than the shelf behind her—some of which she had written herself.

"Where are you when I need you?" Brian asked as he hopped onto a giant stack of books.

"Researching the procedure for centrifuging arthroculus venom and abstracting its precipitates."

"Why?"

"Because science demands it!" the professor whispered as loudly as she could. To Professor Chaff, talking loudly in a place as sacred as a library bordered on blasphemy. "Did you want something, boy?"

In just a few minutes, Brian explained his thoughts on Yenny's perilous situation to the professor.

"So, you know that a world-class criminal, possibly a client of a powerful criminal group, is going to a heavily populated city, and you want me to take you there?" The look in Professor Chaff's eyes was as good as a hearty *no*. "Go home and wait for—ARE YOU STANDING ON MY NEW BOOKS?!"

Brian ran for it, right past the grumpy receptionist and down the stairs that led outside, where a concerned Alasha was walking up the steps. She stopped and waited for Brian's response. He took a deep breath and prepared to deliver the bad news.

"She said we can go whenever we're ready. She wants us to do whatever it takes to help Yenny," he told her.

Brian had considered coming up with a lie to get Alasha to stay safely in town, where there were people everywhere; but he still had not forgotten the fear he'd felt at seeing Alasha strung up in a tree. And truth be told, he was her only friend outside of school, as she mostly stuck to herself. Brian wanted Alasha to stay with him, so he could protect her from harm.

"We? Why *we*? What is she doing?" Alasha asked skeptically.

"Professor Chaff said she wants to alert the guardians first. She even said we could take her hippoverd." He pointed to Professor Chaff's steed, which was tethered to a nearby pole and digging its longest horn into the ground.

"Have you tamed one?" Alasha asked.

"How hard can it be?" Brian said confidently.

However, it was a very rocky start, for Brian hadn't known hippoverds were magical. When frightened, they would unleash blasts of air from their rear ends, rocketing forward. Three times Brian was dragged across the grass at high speeds, trying pull the hippoverd forward with the reins while being covered in smelly gases he did not want to know about.

"Let me have a try," said Alasha at last, destroying the word "try" in the process. She grabbed the reins from Brian's hand and patted the beast, which knelt immediately so that Alasha could get on.

"Okay, cool. Let's leave," a dirt-covered, windswept Brian suggested. He jumped on behind Alasha, and they rode out into the street.

A few groups of people strolling through town recognized them and shouted greetings, most likely thinking Brian and Alasha were on their way to the market—not leaving the town to face a Raider.

Vennisburg had no official physical boundary besides the long brown fields that were ready for harvest out past the Flaming Forest, so Brian wasn't certain when they left the town's limits. He and Alasha looked backward at the town growing small behind them, where the tallest buildings were only three stories and the trees and clouds had fire of their own.

"I never been to a big city before," Alasha said. "Does Shiroho like people like me?" she asked nervously.

"Alasha, most people in Shiroho are Falcons. Every knows Falcons are extroverts who party and talk to everyone. You've got nothing to worry about. Promise."

"What about you?" Alasha asked. "How do you feel?"

"I feel fantastic," Brian said. And he meant it, for Brian had finally figured out what he wanted, and why. In one week, he had experienced the most excitement he ever had. Then, just as quickly as it had come, it had ended. What were the odds of another big-eared kid flying into him? Now that Brian knew what it felt like to be the center of attention and adventure, he couldn't just pass it up so easily.

It was true that Brian did not particularly like Yenny. And while Brian did not wish the kid any harm, he wasn't particularly concerned about the Raider who was most likely tracking him. But taking on Mamlith and running across a Raider had made Brian feel something that not even money could: It had made him feel as though he could do absolutely anything. Perhaps if Brian found Yenny again, he could become a hero in whatever situation Yenny would get himself involved with next.

"Brian, look!" Alasha said, pointing excitedly ahead.

Brian squinted and could barely make out a cart on wheels down the road. Beside it, a man was fixing wires on a large white machine.

Skeptical, Brian followed Alasha, and they approached the cart. Alasha leaned forward to inspect the contraption.

"Is that an ice machine?" Alasha asked hopefully.

"Sure is," the man said. "Shipped straight from Blitzland. They're always making fancy new electrical stuff. We're out of drinks at the moment, until I get this fixed. All I have is ice!"

"Yes, that's exactly what I want!" Alasha said with glee.

The man looked at her more closely. "Ah, Touketian. Help yourself," he said. The man opened the freezer door, revealing blocks of ice. Alasha put her hands on the ice, and Brian heard many *cracks* as the ice broke under Alasha's touch. She brought her hands out, and dozens of shards of white ice followed and surrounded her like flies.

"Where are you going to keep all that?" Brian asked.

"In here with my earrings," Alasha said. She opened her bag, and all of the floating ice flew neatly inside. Brian noticed that not a single piece of ice hit the ground, and remembered his own lousy, clumsy work with the earth.

It seemed like they rode forever. Brian did his best not to be bored, but it was hard when the only thing he could focus on was the increasing soreness of his backside from riding the hippoverd.

Many hours later, they reached a fork in the road. To the right, the skyline of a large city dominated the landscape. Alasha opened her damp bag and refroze the ice. A large collection of clumsily stacked, rusty huts blocked the way, but it was still obviously the shortest way to go.

"Why we going left?" Alasha asked as Brian pulled the hippoverd to the left. "I can see the city."

"Look closer," Brian said, pointing at the boxes, which he could now see had cut-out windows. Though Brian couldn't make out anything in particular, vague figures could be seen in the dark, lightless interiors. Even from this distance, the stench was unmistakable.

"They're malkin slums," Brian said. "This road goes right through them. Better to go around and get to Shiroho late than go through."

A year previously, Brian might have made a different decision. However, malkins were lately becoming an increasing problem. As astromy use decreased, they were becoming braver and venturing out more. There were half-proven stories of how they used human skulls for bowls, and the other bones for decorating their homes.

Brian coughed. The smell had gotten even stronger, as if malkins were right behind them—

Brian turned his head first, and then Alasha. They didn't even have the courage to gasp as they had their first up-close look at a malkin. The sight was overwhelming; there were five of them.

The first thing Brian noticed was that they all carried giant stone clubs that appeared more than capable of knocking a person out cold. The next thing he noticed was how ugly the malkins were. They were humanoid ghouls with greenish-brown skin, crooked yellow teeth, and featureless black eyes. Their nails were overgrown and covered with dirt, and their curly gray hair grew in odd places such as the sides of their faces, above their elbows, and even on their teeth. Most of their outfits seemed clumsily stitched together, but one malkin was definitely wearing human clothes. Malkins had been known to occasionally allow humans to pass safely through their territory if offered clothes, but they were more likely to snatch the garments away so aggressively that body parts came with them.

"Vennisburg pups," said the closest one. If frogs could talk, Brian thought, they would sound like malkins. They spoke with croaks and had reptilian walks. Brian could already confirm one rumor; a malkin in the back was drinking from what was left of a skull.

"Jagger want girl. Jagger want queen," said the malkin with the skull. His voice was low and gravelly. The closest malkin grabbed Alasha's upper arm and pulled her closer. "Don't want him."

The malkins advanced with their bats raised. Brian could tell they were excited from the constant croaking they were making. But that wasn't important. Alasha was in danger, and Brian needed to fight off these three malkins with whatever earth astromy he could muster.

Alasha bit the fingers of the malkin holding her, and it screamed and let go. She pulled her hand out of her bag, and a sheet of ice flew into the nearest malkin's face, blinding him.

The malkin roared like a bull, punching the air wildly until it hit another malkin. Three of them ran toward Alasha, who threw balls of ice at their feet. The ice erupted, and the malkins were trapped.

The stinking malkin holding Brian let go as well, and ran at Alasha with his club. Brian scrambled to his feet to go to Alasha's aid, but it turned out he didn't have to.

Alasha made a small ice shield, which she raised to block. The ice shield reformed around her hand, and she grabbed the malkin's throat. The creature squealed and fell to its knees. Brian saw an icy handprint on its throat where Alasha's hand had been.

"Get up," Alasha said, grabbing a very stunned Brian.

They had just reached the hippoverd when a malkin lunged for Alasha. It missed, but grabbed onto her bag. The fabric ripped, and all of Alasha's ice and earrings fell out. Alasha kicked the malkin in the shin as she jumped onto the panicking hippoverd. Once she was seated securely, Brian jumped up behind her.

"Get us out of here!" Brian cried.

The hippoverd galloped past the malkins, who were whacking each other without any sign of stopping.

"Not through the slums, not through the slums!" Brian cried as he tried to gain control of the hippoverd. But it was no good;

it rode into the alleyway through the shadows of the giant square stacks in the slums. But through the slums they went, splashing through puddles of dirty water and dipping down dark gray alleys so tight, Brian couldn't even stretch his arms out.

By now, malkins had appeared by the dozens, in various shapes and hues, some jumping from rooftops and others scampering on all fours on the filthy ground, smashing through walls and jumping out of garbage piles to surround the strangers. Brian and Alasha rode into a very small square. In the claustrophobic space, a pile of dead animals lay rotting. The hippoverd struggled to stop itself before it slammed into the stained wall of a hut. They looked around and saw they were completely surrounded.

"I need new skull!" a malkin croaked, blocking one exit.

"I want more shiny treasure," said a dirtier one, holding one of the earrings that had fallen out of Alasha's bag.

Malkins scurried on the ground and jumped on the rooftops, howling and beating the roofs with sticks like monkeys. They were ready for a show—one they'd probably seen many times before.

The hippoverd stomped the dirt in a last stand. Alasha was out of ice, and Brian didn't know what to do. He still didn't know how to do astromy!

Brian remembered how he had struggled fighting against the Raider, how he had accidently kept attracting that large rock to himself.

"Alasha, I've got an idea," Brian said. He jumped down and slammed his hands to the muddy ground. The malkins, seeing that Brian was prepared to fight, charged forward before several crashes echoed through the night.

Rocks the size of hippoverds broke out of the street and came straight toward Brian, exactly as the rock had that day he had been practicing with Professor Chaff and Yenny. Technically, he was still making a mistake, but it worked in his favor this time. He hadn't learned how to properly do astromy yet, but that could wait.

"You learned how to use earth," Alasha said, shocked.

"Technically, I'm doing it wrong," Brian said as he jumped onto the hippoverd. He and Alasha rode through the dispersing crowd. The astromized stones broke half the shacks to pieces as they followed Brian. But even now, Brian and Alasha had one last barricade of approaching malkins to run through.

"Take this!" Brian yelled as he kicked his ankles into the hippoverd's side. A *boom* from the hippoverd's rear end rocketed them all forward through the wall of malkins, sending the creatures flying into the air and landing in what remained of their slums.

"That was awesome!" Brian cried as he turned to face Alasha. "How did you get so good at ice astromy? That was amazing."

"I spent my whole life around ice," Alasha said. "Eventually you just pick it up."

"Oh," was all Brian said as they continued riding. If she could do that with just a handful of ice, Brian wondered how powerful Alasha would be in Touket during one of their many snowfalls.

"Pull over now!" Alasha said as they got closer to a nearby pond. Alasha jumped off and ran over, submerging her head into the water.

"What are you doing?" Brian asked as she came up for air.

"I *bit* a malkin. There's malkin germs and hair in my teeth," Alasha said. She took a big gulp, rinsed her mouth, and spat, then ran her fingers across her gums. "Oh, I'm going to die from malkin germs!"

Shiroho City

The city of Shiroho gradually came into view. It looked to Brian and Alasha like a collection of gigantic cones stacked on top of each other. As they came closer, Brian heard loud voices and the constant roar of flames.

"There's a volcano?" Alasha asked. She pointed to a mountain that towered behind the city. A pile of smoke rose from it.

"Yeah, that's Mount Shiroho," Brian said, shifting slightly so he could get a good look at Alasha. "Don't worry; it hasn't been active in years. Are you ready to see the city?"

"We should get to the Angelus first and warn him that Yenny may be in danger from the Raider, remember?" Alasha said.

"Oh, yeah," Brian said, avoiding eye contact.

The sun was reaching the final stages of its curve in the sky as Brian and Alasha reached the outskirts of Shohiro City. The road they had taken in from the country led through a giant open iron gate. Flanking the entrance were white flags bearing yellow circles with red triangles inside: symbols representing the Fire Falcon, the constellation that gave fire astromers their powers.

"'Fly with burning passion'?" Alasha read one of the flags.

"It's the Falcon catchphrase," Brian answered. "Like how the Swan one is . . . something about peace, right?"

"We do not find peace, we make it!" Alasha said proudly.

About a mile into the city, they came across a stable that would care for their mount overnight for just a few coins. Then, with only their packs on their backs, Brian and Alasha walked toward the city center, taking in the majesty of the capital.

"What do you think of the buildings?" Brian asked Alasha, pointing to the giant cone-shaped towers. "Dwarves always build weird buildings like these."

Alasha said nothing, but stared quietly around her, her head turning from side to side. She seemed to have forgotten why they had come.

Many of the children Brian saw had red beads strung around their necks, and teenagers seemed to prefer unicycles to walking. Many young children had falcons printed on their shirts, and they even saw one with a falcon-shaped backpack, and two wearing falcon hats. Many adults wore hats with a falcon's feather sticking out, or vests with feathers attached to the back in winglike designs.

And there were astromers! Brian had never seen so many astromers in one place, but he figured their presence in the capital was to be expected. Astromers tended to move to cities in search of more jobs and activities that suited their talents. Shohiro's astromers seemed to be mostly fire-based. Brian peered into a local bakery to see a baker put his bare hands into an oven and carry out a handful of flames.

Fire was universally the most common form of astromy, and Brian felt it was the most practical, as it could be used for heating, lighting, melting, and cooking. The biggest downside was that fire astromy was hard to master in freezing cold or rain. Just like any other element, an astromer had to physically touch the fire in order to transfer enough energy for the flames to be controlled. He or she could only hold the flames for so long before they burned out.

"Brian, hold up a second," Alasha said excitedly. "I want to buy pyroses." Alasha pointed to a large floral shop nearby that had falcons flying back and forth through the shop's windows.

Pyroses looked like glowing flowers, but the petals were magical flames that grew at the end of dark green stems. They gave off powerful aromas reminiscent of harvests and gardens, making Brian want to fall asleep.

"Make sure to brush those embers off. They'll grow into pyrose bushes anywhere," the seller called to Alasha as she walked away with a whole bouquet of flower-shaped fire, bringing the blooms as close as possible to her nose. She was giving them so much attention that she almost walked into a pair of astromers. The astromers lumbered around on stilts that were on fire, and one of them juggled fire over the eager crowd's heads.

"Brian, let's go to the Landing!" Alasha said, looking at a map on a wooden post right outside the floral shop.

Dwarf's Landing was the name of the bay where dwarves had first landed centuries ago, after voyaging here from the other side of the world. It had never become clear what had happened to them, but they'd left their dwarven ships.

Alasha had to leave the pyroses at the gate with the coordinator before she and Brian were allowed to squeeze in through the tiny door and hunch their way through the halls, gawk at cages used for criminals, make their way through the cramped sleeping quarters, and crouch in the captain's room, where they pretended to use the strange telescopes before being hurried out to make room for the next group of tourists.

"Ooooh, oh my gosh! Brian! Let's go to—"

"For crying out loud, Alasha! You said yourself, we're not on vacation!"

But Alasha had found her dream spot: the Mappahannock Zoo, which was perfect for Alasha's animal craze. It was so big that trains offered rides to the other side. Alasha ran back and forth, dragging Brian along as she pointed out all the animals.

"Those are *divvips*!" She pointed to animals with horse bodies and duck heads. "Only females have the tails, see? And those are *raijus*." Alasha pointed to a pack of black hounds with yellow stripes. "They're native to Blitzland and their bites give you electric shocks. Oh, look, they let you go in. Let's go!"

Brian and Alasha were allowed in only after being checked for any water or metal they might have been carrying. They took turns patting the raijus, feeling static electricity popping in the creatures' fur. By the time Brian and Alasha left the raiju cage, the hair on their heads was puffed up all over the place from the static electricity.

"We're doing that," Alasha said as she pointed to a sign that said DECAPEDE CHALLENGE. "Come on, Brian! If we ride one, we get a prize."

Brian peeped over the crowd of people curiously while asking, "What are . . . ?" But his curiosity turned to disgust when he saw the decapede. The good news was that it didn't appear to have a mouth; but it was still a giant black wormlike creature, with orange legs and a mighty pair of pincers at its rear.

But Brian grabbed her and walked her to the front of the line of people waiting for the Decapede Challenge. Nobody tried to stop Brian and Alasha from cutting, and some actually seemed to prefer they go first.

"You'll be fine," Alasha said. "Imagine it's one of those things that go *choo choo*."

"You mean trains? What trains do you know that go up those?" Brian said, pointing down brown path toward a clearing. The path was ridiculously structured in bizarre patterns that covered half the zoo. Many hills went straight up to the sky, and there were even vertical loops that literally left the ground and curved backward into circles. The area looked less like a zoo and more like a roller coaster park.

"Do they want to send us to the hospital?" asked Brian as he and Alasha climbed onto the decapede's back. The animal felt like a prickly water bed that shifted under their weight. It was a lot stickier than Brian had expected, which probably helped to keep people from falling off.

A young lady in a burgundy vest spoke loudly at the decapede's head for the two to hear. "Welcome aboard the Decapede Challenge. The path before you was built to replicate the style of the streets often found in dwarf cities. For your safety, please remain seated at all times, keep your arms and legs to yourself, don't pull out the decapede's hairs, don't sit or slide between the pincers, and do not throw food or trash. One passenger last year threw an empty cup at the decapede's head and sent everyone to the hospital for three weeks. Thanks, and enjoy the ride!"

The decapede bolted with almost no warning. It slowly gained speed, passing all the buildings and the other decapedes, and soon everything became a blur. Brian and Alasha bounced up and down on the bumpy ride. The giant decapede sped up as it approached the first loop.

"No, please, don't," Brian squealed. His complaint escalated to a scream as they entered the loop. All sense of direction was lost, and the world spun before Brian's eyes until he decided to keep them shut.

"I didn't expect this!" Alasha yelled.

"Alasha, get ready! We're about to go on interlocking loops!"

"Noooooo!" Alasha cried.

Brian felt his own body was likely to slip off. He grabbed the decapede's hairs tighter and screamed alongside Alasha. He couldn't tell which way was up or where they were—until suddenly, it was over.

"Welcome back! Please use the green trash cans to vomit, then come up and claim your prize! Four free-for-one-night passes to any of our Resting Falcon Hotel locations in the world!" yelled the decapede attendant, amid the claps of the crowd.

It took Brian a moment to stand, as his legs were still wobbling. "That wasn't too bad," he said.

"Yes, quite fun," Alasha replied, a slight shade of green. Both of them tried to laugh, then ran to the green trash can to vomit.

"Are you serious? There's a tower just for me?" Yenny yelled over the wind.

"It's not specifically for you," Master Paleo corrected. "It was built for the use of all the Day Kings. There it is in front of us."

Yenny saw a tall tower of stone on a gorgeous green island surrounded by sea. Yenny saw a heard of pure white deer with golden horns eating grass close to the water.

"Close your eyes, Yenny. We have to ascend."

Yenny shut his eyes tight and held his breath as Supersonic Airmaster swooped up a rocky cliff on the side of the island. Supersonic Airmaster lifted its wings and landed smoothly on the ground.

"Welcome to Celestial Tower," Master Paleo said, sliding off of Supersonic Airmaster and launching immediately into a series of stretches for his legs, arms, and back. While Yenny inspected the landscape, Master Paleo performed lunges, then ran in place for a few seconds.

"Okay, I'm all done," he called to Yenny and Fireworks, who had been exploring the grounds in wonder.

Yenny had seen both the blue ocean and fruit trees before. But there was something different about the ocean, trees, and sky here. Everything Yenny laid eyes on seemed to be filled with magic; the colors, the rays of light, and even the air were richer. He could feel the light dripping over his skin like oil, and the air rushing between his fingers was nearly tangible. The ocean's waves, though several miles below, seemed just a finger's length away, and its spray found his nostrils even at this height.

"It's like everything I'm seeing is breathing," Yenny said to Fireworks.

Looking around, he saw the park was filled with more of the kingdeer he had seen down below, as well as with a variety of trees. Yenny recognized one.

"That's a tree from the Flaming Forest!" Yenny said, walking toward it. This tree bore the telltale pine cones that lit up at night.

"They're the national star trees," Paleo said. "Each nation has a national constellation, planet, tree, and animal. Remember?"

"What about that tree?" Yenny pointed to a tree that looked like it was made of metal on the other side of the field. A distinctive popping sound could be heard from its black leaves.

"That's a pole tree. That's the national tree of Blitzland, where the Lightning Leopard shines brightest. Please don't touch that unless you want electricity sent all through your body."

Yenny turned to look back at the tower, and for the first time noticed the gray statue of a tall, muscular krystee with hair down his back to his hips. Two shiny amethysts represented the eyes. On the statue's back was the sheath containing a giant sword, and at its feet, in the middle of a pentagon-shaped pool, a mighty fire burned on top of the water. Not on a log, or on rocks—it truly burned on the water itself.

Master Paleo led the way to the top of the stone stairs and pushed the doors open. Although the tower had been without a king for almost two millennia, it was still more than fit to live in. The outside walls bore no ivy, and the lawns weren't overgrown; the inside was clear of dust, neat and tidy. Stone stairs spiraled from the floor all the way to the ceiling. The only light came from the sun shining through the tower's large windows, but at this time of day, it was more than enough.

At the end of the entrance hall was a large chair, which looked more like a throne. When Yenny jumped onto it, he bounced a little, his toes far from touching the floor.

"Master Paleo, is all this really for me?" asked Yenny with a big grin on his face. He had no real memory of his past, unless he counted the laughing, faceless man in the shadows of his mind. Yenny had spent almost a year wandering with Master Paleo without having any idea that he had a house—a humongous, ancient, magical house.

"Yes, but I did not call you here to take in the decorations," said Master Paleo urgently. He walked backed outside, his staff tapping every time it hit the floor. Yenny jumped off the throne and followed, leaving Fireworks behind to scamper around.

"To put it bluntly, Yenny," said Master Paleo, "the world is changing faster than ever. We have trains that can carry people across land masses, and ships so strong they can take you across the seas. The last time I visited Blitzland, I saw them working on machines that can carry people through the air. However, a lot of bad things have been happening as well."

"You mean like less cake?"

"Well, that too. But I was mostly talking about the increase in malkins. Not too long ago, they spawned away in their dens and slums, rarely coming out into the sunlight. But now, they are starting to leave their territory and venture forth. It's not just malkins; minotaurs, werewolves, and other beasts have been encroaching on civilized places. Not to mention the dark wizards who can control them. Once you are crowned Day King, it will be your job to tend to all of these matters."

Yenny's mind produced a multitude of pictures: countless faces and nameless beasts he must defeat, their glowing eyes and saliva-drowned tongues salivating for him, ready to challenge the world's king. A silent, dark-green-armored thing that would hunt him forever. This was starting to sound even worse than a world with no cake.

"I suppose my main concern is that the world is not ready for a Day King right now," Master Paleo continued. "It would require unity, which is something we are lacking. But what you need is your symbol, something no one will question; and I am not talking about crowns and mantles. Something that is right in front of our eyes. In that fire."

Yenny strained his eyes and saw it. In the middle of the fire was an actual sword!

Yenny marveled at how the sword stood there in the very heat of the flame without melting. "Is that the same sword that's on the krystee's back. The one outside?" Yenny asked.

"That statue wasn't modeled after any normal krystee," said Paleo. "In fact, some would say he hardly counted as a krystee. That krystee was none other than Day King Titan."

"Titan? *The* Titan? You mean the Day King that lived two thousand years ago?" asked Yenny. He had paid the statue little attention before, but now walked closer to see more of it. Everyone knew Titan, not just because he was the last Day King, but because the feats he had accomplished when he was alive were legendary.

"The very same," said Master Paleo with a nod. "He was renowned as the greatest Day King of all time. He's the one who fought against the Great Night Lord and threw his armies back, leading us to victory in the War of the Keys. He also stayed away from sweets and ate vegetables and fruits—just saying.

"After the final battle, Day King Titan disappeared without a trace. It has been said that he lost something very important to him and died from grief."

"Who made that sword?" asked Yenny. He had listened to the story while inspecting every inch of the statue.

"You really want to know the answer to that question?" Master Paleo waited for Yenny to nod. "The sword itself belongs to none other than Theo, the Father of Stars."

"You mean Theo told someone to make the sword?"

"No. The sword was made by Theo himself, with his own hands—the same hands that turn time."

"He made this *himself?*" shouted Yenny as he backed away from the sword. At first, Yenny had seen the sword as an awesome relic or a cool toy to play with. But now, the sword seemed far too great for him. This sword had to be more powerful than anything, even Day King Titan himself.

"That's right. And Theo didn't speak the sword into existence or snap his fingers. He descended from the heavens and made this blade through his own hard work. You can relax. This sword is inside your tower for a reason," said Master Paleo.

"Which is?" asked Yenny.

"In the first days, the world was empty, nothing but shadows and ice everywhere. Then Theo appeared, and on the very first day, he gave us light. Theo was the very first star, and it was he who watched and guided the universe during its creation. However, the only world he shaped with his own hands was this world; that is why we humans are so special. He brought understanding to humankind and gave us speech. He was perfect, and yet he loved us and wanted to be loved in return.

"But love wasn't enough for us. We turned against him. In our pride, we tried to take his place, and soon even the beasts rebelled against him. Due to humankind's fall, Theo was forced to leave the world, taking only the nine most faithful with him: the falcon, the wyvern, the swan, the whamopus, the fox, the elephant, the leopard, the lion, and the snake. He rewarded them by turning them into the Great Constellations we use today, giving them free reign to dictate their favorite personality traits when they shined the brightest."

"So those nine animals became the reason astromy was created?" Yenny asked, amazed. "But what does that have to do with the sword?"

"When Theo left, the world was cast into eternal night again," Paleo continued. "But there were still people who were loyal to him and wished for him to stay. When he refused, the people asked him to choose a leader. A leader they could see and touch, who had Theo's wisdom and power. And so Theo chose the very first Basileus, or Great King. On the day the Basileus was born, Theo created the sun, the closest star to our planet, to start the very first day. From that day forth, the Basileus would be known to many as the Day King.

"But the first Basileus didn't like the idea very much. He feared the responsibility and worried that his family would be in danger if he accepted. To comfort him, Theo promised to give him a piece of his own power manifested in physical form. While that person's name has long since been forgotten, a long line of kings, including Day King Titan, have used this sword to show his wonders. This is why we're here."

Yenny's deep purple eyes met Paleo's dark, timeworn ones. If what Master Paleo said was true, then he would soon be wielding the most powerful weapon ever made.

"So you think this sword is—"

"Not think. Know," said Master Paleo, waving his hand in the sword's direction.

Yenny stepped toward the fire, wondering what would happen. This sword had been made by the same hands that had sculpted the stars themselves. Would fire come from the sky, or the seas turn into blood? And what of Yenny himself? In his mind, he imagined himself standing over everyone, wielding some of the same power that had placed each star in the sky, his eyes glowing fiercely like purple suns, and his orders echoing to the farthest white mountaintop.

Yenny stepped into the pool, forgetting to take off his shoes or roll up his pants. Walking forward, he became aware of his breathing. He stood there, staring at the sword, noticing how the flames swirled around it like a sheath. "What if I get burned?"

"The Sword won't burn the Day King."

Yenny reached out and grabbed the hilt. It was silver and decorated with amethysts that glowed like purple stars. The moment his fingers touched the metal, orange flames roared around him.

Gone were the sun, the trees, and Master Paleo. Yenny now stood in what appeared to be an ancient room with cracks zigzagging through the brown walls and cobwebs clinging to the corners. The only light came from the torches that were lit in each corner. He supposed he was underground, because the ceiling was laced with tree roots.

In the shadows of the darkest corner of the room, standing side by side, were two people: a man and a woman, each wearing plain white robes.

"Pick up the sword," said the woman. She had such command in her voice that Yenny didn't even think about disobeying. He grabbed the sword and yanked it upward again. Once again, nothing happened.

"I predicted this," the woman seethed. "I told you he would grow into this. I knew from the moment I gave birth to him."

"You didn't give birth to me. I never met you," Yenny said.

The man and woman stepped forward in unison, and Yenny saw their faces. They were krystees; Yenny could tell by the woman's ears and the man's red eyes. In fact, they looked strangely familiar. The male krystee had a chin Yenny recognized, but his facial hair made it hard to place him. His long black hair hung braided down the middle of his back. On the woman's face, Yenny saw his own nose, his cheeks, and the exact same lips.

Yenny stood there, shocked, for a moment that seemed to last forever. Then, coming to his senses, he ran faster than he had ever run in his life toward his parents. Who cared about a sword or being king? This was what Yenny had wanted for six years: his own mother and father.

Yenny got just close enough to see their eyes when he was knocked backward by an invisible force and sent rolling across the floor. This time, it wasn't because he had tripped. He'd been hit in the face by his father's fist.

"She told you to pick that up," Yenny's father said impatiently, pointing to the sword.

"Don't you recognize me?" Yenny begged. "I'm your son."

"You're no son of mine. I raised a king, not a coward."

Before Yenny could do more than whimper, more people walked slowly out of the dark hallways. They were people Yenny recognized from Vennisburg.

"A king?" laughed a medicist from the clinic, her hands and scrubs covered in blood.

"Kids have to grow up sometime. You're no king," Professor Chaff mocked, her glasses shattered and opaque.

"I am the Day King," Yenny yelled.

They were all closing in, taunting and jeering, his mother and father in front; and it was they who laughed the hardest. They both spoke together: "We have no king. We don't even have a son."

"Yenny!"

In a blink, there was Master Paleo. Yenny realize he was shaking, probably because he was soaking wet. He had fallen into the pool, and by the looks of it, had splashed and rolled all over the place.

"Come sit over here," Master Paleo said, sitting him down on the green grass. His hands glowed with light as he pressed them against Yenny's clothes, and Yenny felt his master's astromy steadily evaporating the water from his back and sleeves.

"What did you see?" Master Paleo asked. "Did you have a vision?"

"I don't know," Yenny gasped. "What happened?"

"The fire engulfed you, and you started screaming. I thought you'd been burned at first. What did you see?"

Yenny did not answer immediately. How on earth was he supposed to explain his terrible vision? Instead, he asked a question. "Master Paleo, what can you tell me about my parents?"

"Well, not much that I haven't told you already. I believe your father is one of the leaders of the krystee community that lives near Bosque Forest."

"But you said you couldn't find any information on that."

"And that's precisely why. Krystee leaders and their families are kept in secrecy. There were at least five krystees who could've been your father, and we aren't even sure of their names. As for your mother, I have absolutely nothing."

"But I'm sure they talked about me."

"Yenny, I never met your parents. Let's eat something."

"I'm not very hungry," Yenny said.

"That's it. Tell me what's wrong with you at once, Yenitus!" Paleo demanded, standing up. "You have ten seconds."

Yenny hesitated. He wanted to tell Paleo how he'd been so sure that his parents wanted to meet him. He wanted to tell Paleo how he'd hoped that if he ever found his parents, they would tell him they'd been looking for him everywhere, and that they loved him so very much. But most of all, Yenny wanted to tell Master Paleo how no one had believed him when he'd told them he was the king.

On the other hand, if he told Master Paleo all this, Paleo might think that Yenny was weak and unworthy of the sword. But then again, Yenny had already taken an awfully long time to answer the question.

"I saw my parents," Yenny said.

"That's excellent!" Paleo said, dropping his staff in surprise. "Theo granted you a vision of your heart's desire! What did they say to you?"

"Master Paleo, did you ever try to be something you didn't deserve to be?"

"Hmm. Well, I tried to be sad once. I was having a very bad day, and I thought I deserved to be miserable."

"I mean something good you didn't deserve," Yenny said.

"Why would I not deserve something good?" Paleo asked.

Yenny was ready to give a defeated "Never mind"—but instead, he glanced at the sun. Yenny usually knew better than to look at the sun, for of course, it could blind a person. However, he felt an irresistible pull toward the great yellow orb in the sky, and against his better judgment, he looked directly at it. It seemed to beat like a yellow, living heart. Was that how the sun was supposed to look? Looking at it filled Yenny with awe, and he felt his heart was beating along with sun, the synchronized beat filling him with ease.

At last, Yenny said, "When I was in Vennisburg, I tried to tell people I was the Day King. It's the same thing that happened in Mokan. No matter what happens or what I do, no one believes me."

"Don't listen to your doubters more than you listen to your own dreams."

"But everyone says the same thing. They always laugh at me,

even my new friends. They can't all be wrong."

"People believe many things that are not true, and many never believe in anything at all. But know you have at least one person who believes in you."

"But what if I can't do it?"

"You can."

"I know, but—what if I *can't?*"

"Well, maybe *we* can." Master Paleo pulled Yenny to his feet and walked him over to the pool. As Yenny and Paleo cautiously waded in, water squished its way once more into Yenny's shoes.

"You have to touch the sword first," Master Paleo said.

Yenny grabbed the hilt, and Master Paleo's larger hands surrounded his.

"On the count of three, Yenny. One . . . two . . . three—!"

Together they pulled. A great crack stopped Yenny's heart, and a cry resonated through the air.

15

Malcolm's Secret

The castle of Shiroho had the marks of dwarves all over it. Years of surviving as nomadic hunter-gatherers had given dwarves nimble fingers that they used to finesse small objects. They could sand a stone with incredible precision while blindfolded, and balance asymmetric items for hours. The castle's black stone towers, each topped with a gigantic stone falcon, displayed a tiny fraction of the artistry the dwarves were capable of. Alasha and Brian walked up the stairs, mouths agape.

"This is so humbling. The time they had to put into this!" Alasha said.

Brian, who had never been humble in his life, walked up to the royal wooden door as though the guards would just open it for him.

"You cannot pass beyond this door," said the guard on the left.

"Do you know who I am?" Brian asked casually.

"No," both guards answered.

"I'm only the richest kid in all of Kama. Terith Boulard from Vennisburg? I'm his son." Alasha brought her hand to her forehead in embarrassment.

"Oh! I had no idea!" said a guard with wide eyes. "Would

you like to stay in the castle tonight, courtesy of Kama's finest?"

"Yes, I would!" Brian said, nodding in approval.

"Well, you can't. Never heard of you," one guard said while the other laughed.

"We're heroes!" Brian protested. "We defeated Mamlith, for crying out loud. Why can't we stay in the castle?"

"Come back in five years when you actually do something useful."

As Brian and Alasha turned to leave, Brian heard the unmistakable slap of a high five.

"I think Shiroho has a Resting Falcon Hotel," Brian mumbled, holding his prize from the Decapede Challenge. They walked down the stone steps and back onto the main street. Now that Brian knew he wasn't famous here, the city no longer seemed as exciting.

Brian called for one of the dozens of cycle rickshaws to take them to the hotel. Alasha was excited, as they didn't have any cycling machines in Touket. In five minutes, they had arrived at a very expensive hotel that had a nice view of Mappahannock Bay at the base of Mount Shiroho.

The best thing about the Resting Falcon Hotel was that they offered free cinnamon apple pie drizzled with caramel to their guests on the deck outside. Brian and Alasha looked at their snacks, then at each other, then at the dwarf ships docked in the bay. Brian thought he could see bats flying toward the bay from the direction of the hissing volcano. Near the ships, a large crowd had gathered around a troupe of acrobats, who were performing leaps and rolls dangerously close to what looked like a giant ball of fire.

Once Brian and Alasha had gotten all the excitement of the

city over with, they had remembered why they had come in the first place: to look for Yenny and tell him he might be in trouble. Now that they were where they wanted to be, they had no idea what to do—something Alasha was quick to point out.

"I guess we wait," Brian answered.

It was getting dark, and the city was starting to release occasional fireworks into the sky, reminding Brian of the crackling fireballs that the kid's pet could breathe out.

"What if Yenny doesn't come?" Alasha asked. "He could always have changed his mind about finding the Stones." A floral purple explosion went off in the night sky.

Brian had not considered that. If Yenny was not in Shiroho City, then they were wasting time—and they might not be able to find Yenny again. Even worse, Brian would have wasted his perfectly good money on the hotel and food.

"He'll be here eventually," Brian said at last.

"But what if you not right?" Alasha asked, stumbling over the "R" sound.

"Alasha, we've been through this before. I'm always right!" Brian clapped his hands together. The alternative—Brian being wrong—was impossible, unless he was arguing with Professor Chaff. But Alasha asked the same question again and again. Brian did not want to go back to Vennisburg empty-handed—at least not without a very good excuse he could give to Professor Chaff for running off with her hippoverd. Perhaps Brian could buy some books to bring back that the professor wouldn't be able to find anywhere else, about astromy or malkins.

Professor Chaff had said that malkins originated from humans being exposed to too much astromy, or had otherwise been born from using forbidden astromy in dark practices such as witchcraft. If Brian and Alasha continued to perform astromy, would they turn into malkins eventually? Brian touched his teeth, wondering how long it would take for gray hair to grow. Looking at his fingernails, he realized they were getting a little long. He imagined waking up one day to fingernails that were yellow and curved.

"Did you hear me?" Alasha asked, breaking Brian out of his wonderings.

"Huh?" Brian said. "Whatever it was, I'm right."

"Just look, fool," Alasha said, pointing.

A man was limping toward them; his face was covered in bandages. He leaned heavily on a cane and moved slowly, making him appear either really old or badly hurt. He wore a large coat that seemed inappropriate in the summer evening.

"Is that . . . Malcolm?" Brian asked. It had to be. The figure bore the exact same wrappings that Malcolm had worn in Vennisburg, when he was in the clinic. But what gave his identity away was the brown bat perched on his left shoulder. On his other shoulder, a black traveling bag swung back and forth as he walked.

"Long time no see," Malcolm said joyfully, landing heavily on the chair beside Brian.

"What are you doing here?" Alasha asked, standing up in shock.

"I was discharged from the clinic yesterday, and I couldn't wait to come home," Malcolm grunted, breathing heavily. "No offense, but Vennisburg never struck me as exciting. What are you two doing here? Where's Professor Chaff?"

"She, um, had a meeting," Brian said. "Oh, and we rode through a malkin slum."

"There's a malkin slum around here?" Malcolm asked, his jaw dropping.

Brian shared the whole story about how they had come to save Yenny because they believed that the Raider was pursuing him. Alasha seemed as if she was still too busy being surprised to see Malcolm Jones to hear.

"A malkin slum. I swear, you two give *me* a run for my money," Malcolm stated, clapping his hands together. "You know, I'm not entirely sure I should be asking you this. You're only children."

"And we took care of Mamlith and malkins," Brian pointed out.

"That's true. You two are pretty talented. Very well." Malcom looked around, but all the other hotel patrons were eating their delicious desserts and watching the fireworks. There was too much noise for them to be overheard. "The truth is, I'm looking for something called the Fire Baetylus."

"That's what we're looking for!" Brian said. Alasha's blue eyes opened even wider. "We . . . er . . . wanted to know . . . well—"

"Your business is your business," Malcolm said, lifting his hands into the air. "Anyways, I'm leaving very shortly. I would hate for you two to even try to look for it without adult supervision."

"But we don't know the real spot where the Stone is located," Alasha said.

"I know exactly where it is," Malcolm said. "It's in Mount Shiroho. That's not just a mountain; it's a dormant volcano. There's a path that leads through the lava into its center. The Stone hidden in a room that was designed by dwarves, so there will no doubt be traps."

"Did you hear that?" Brian said excitedly, looking at Alasha. "There's a path that leads straight to it, filled with booby traps! You know what we should do?"

"We needed to forget this whole idea, alert the guardians that a Raider might try to enter the city, and then enjoy a night in the hotel before riding home the next day," Alasha said.

"We need to go straight into the center of the volcano and find the Fire Baetylus ourselves," Brian shot back. The hope in Alasha's face went up in flames.

"So, you want to go into the middle of a volcano filled with lava to find something we have no image of?" Alasha clarified.

"Nothing bad will happen to you while you're with me," Malcolm said firmly. "One of my nurses told me that a Raider attacked you. It would be stupid to do something without my protection."

"That would be great!" Brian said. "Alasha, you can stay here if you want."

"No," Alasha said firmly. "I want to help too!"

"Well, no point wasting time," Malcolm said. He got up slowly from his seat and led them across the patio. People were still having too much fun to notice them. Malcolm limped hurriedly behind the hotel, going toward the volcano that loomed in the distance. In his excitement, Brian was ready to run, but Malcolm wasn't rushing—or perhaps he couldn't, due to his injuries.

They walked into the trees for more than hour before the ground sloped up toward the edge of the volcano. It was simple walking for a while, but the group was soon reduced to half-climbing on the rocky black ground, which was covered in slippery ash.

Brian wondered what he would see. Halls made of gold, perhaps? He imagined solving an ancient riddle that opened a dwarven door, revealing the Fire Baetylus at the pinnacle of a heaping mound of gold and jewels. Maybe there was even a dragon guarding the doors. But that didn't matter, because Brian was sure that he could now take on a dragon with his eyes closed.

"What's that sound?" Alasha asked.

"Er," Brian said. Malcolm shook his head while holding his back, still in pain. "Sounds like a wind chime somewhere."

"Oh," Alasha said, though she didn't look convinced. "Mister Jones, you never told us what you were looking for the Baetylus for," Alasha said.

Malcolm let out a long sigh before answering, as though trying to think of how to phrase his thoughts. "Until very recently, I had a boss who knew a lot about these things. My boss told me a lot about the Baetyli, including where they are located." Malcolm stumbled on a rock, and a jingling could be heard from his bag. "Until I, well, I got fired. I lost my job because of my interest in the Baetyli, actually." Brian thought he heard anger somewhere in Malcolm's voice.

"So, you want the Flame Baetylus because you want job back?" Alasha asked. "Your boss wants the Baetylus?"

"Everyone wants a Baetylus, Alasha. They are all in dangerous places so that they can stay safe, but that doesn't stop people. It's not common knowledge, but the dwarves first sailed here to find the Fire Baetylus. They probably would have succeeded, if the *pypents* hadn't driven them out."

"*Pypents* are in the volcano?" Alasha asked, stopping immediately. "As in giant fire lizards?"

"Alasha, just *relax*," Brian said. "You worry about everything."

Alasha pursed her lips together, and then she broke into sudden laugher. "You're right. We took care of malkins and Mamlith. We have a lot of talent! Oh, no, I just tripped."

Alasha tripped rather clumsily into Malcolm's side. Somehow, her arm ended up in his bag strap.

"Oh, no, sorry!" Alasha said. But Brian saw Alasha purposely grab Malcolm's bag and pull it open. Out fell a sheaf of papers, a compass, and a couple of very shiny items that Brian was almost certain he recognized.

"Alasha!" Brian said.

But Alasha had already reached down and grabbed the shiny, jingling items. "I made these earlier today!" she said, holding the metal chains up. "They have been jingling in your pocket the whole time."

"They're from another Touketian I met on the way," Malcolm said.

"Was it my mother? She's the only one who makes jewelry like this," Alasha said, waving around a large earring she had made. Brian remembered them. He also remembered that all the jewelry Alasha had lovingly handmade had been dropped in the malkin slums they had passed through earlier.

Brian and Alasha stared at Malcolm, and it was difficult to read the expression on his quiet, bandaged face.

"How did you get these?" Alasha asked. "Malkins don't just give away jewelry. You always said you would never walk into malkin slums."

"You have to answer my question first," Malcolm answered in a quiet voice. "Have you ever seen Mamlith? I never got an answer that day. What do you think he looks like? Tall, short?"

"Why does that matter now?" asked Brian.

"If I were you, I would want to know the face of someone who was very, *very* mad at me—perhaps even seeking revenge," Malcolm said. He now stood up straighter, his fingers outstretched as though he was about to reach for something. "He could be standing right beside you, and you wouldn't know until it was too late."

Alasha gasped and jumped backward. Brian saw Malcom take out a dagger, but couldn't react in time. Malcolm dropped his walking stick and lunged for Brian, wrapping one arm around the boy's neck and raising the dagger to Brian's throat with the other hand.

"You! *You're* Mamlith?" Brian said, wildly trying to break away from his grasp.

"Thought you saw the last of me?" Malcom hissed in a voice that matched the rumbling of the volcano.

Brian tried to grab Mamlith's arms, but his own arms were weak and childish compared to the other man's. Underneath Mamlith's jacket, Brian felt that his skin was like very thick, wrinkled paper. Mamlith gave a yelp of pain but didn't let go.

"Easy, boy," Mamlith said through gritted teeth. "It'll be months before my skin heals over."

"But I thought you gone?" said Alasha, who had distanced herself from Mamlith's reach.

"I fell into the cellar when my Baetylus backfired on me," Mamlith spat. Now that he had dropped the fake voice of Malcolm Jones, Brian found it much easier to hear Mamlith's manner of talking. "Imagine every inch of your skin is on fire, being torn away from your bones. I thought I had finally been caught, but thankfully no one suspected that I was Mamlith, and I was carried away for treatment. Speaking of which, thank you for telling me where the Fire Baetylus is located while I was recovering in the clinic. I'm still in a bit of a tight spot, you see? No Baetylus, no Red Robes, and a boss that's after my head. But then you *brilliant* children gave me a wonderful idea: come to Shiroho City and take the Fire Baetylus. Thankfully I managed to catch one of my camazots that had escaped, and I flew here with several of my young winged friends." Mamlith nodded toward the bat that had previously been on his shoulder, and that now flew in circles above them. "They scouted the city for me and managed to find the passage to the Fire Baetylus. Although, I didn't expect to have the pleasure of having them find you two as well." He squeezed his arm harder around Brian's neck.

"Why are you doing this?" Brian asked, still struggling to understand how Mamlith could be the man he had looked up to so much, whom he had seen helping the townsfolk. "We're supposed to be friends! You saved us from the Red Robes when they came over!"

"I wasn't *saving* you," Mamlith said, chuckling. "I train my dogs to work, not play. Harassing children while they should have been keeping the town under control and keeping watch for the Day King. It was an embarrassment."

"But you've been helping people for months," Brian continued. "You brought people who lost their homes into your place."

"I have been spying on the Ember Region for months. Partly because the Day King was rumored to be nearby, and partly because I was promised my own city to rule once I had delivered him to my master. So I befriended Vennisburg to gain their trust and hear their news. You're the only astromer in hundreds of miles; I thought it might be you. But that's all behind us now; we must look to the future. And I foresee all three of us going on a little trip to get the Baetylus. Without it, I have nowhere to go. My master won't forgive me. I'm taking the Fire Baetylus, and then I'll ambush the krystee to get the Light Baetylus back. I won't need your town anymore. And if I can get one more, perhaps I won't need Lord Elyon either."

"Elyon's your master?" Brian asked, so shocked he stopped struggling against Mamlith. "*The* Elyon? Isn't he dangerous?"

"You don't think I'm dangerous?" Mamlith questioned, holding the knife tighter against Brian's throat.

"I just meant, what does he want with Vennisburg?" Brian asked quickly. "Elyon's supposed to be an evil lunatic. They say he's the most powerful wizard in the world. Shouldn't he be going after big cities with important people? So why Vennisburg?"

"Tell you what," Mamlith responded. "Let's get the Baetyli and take them to him. Then you can ask him yourself. Move up that path, girl!"

"Why us?" asked Alasha. "You know where it's hidden. Go get it yourself."

"As we all now know, the Baetyli can be dangerous to use. I won't make the same mistake twice."

"So, you gonna to make me do it?" Alasha asked.

"We always have choice," Mamlith said, the knife now cutting Brian's neck.

"Okay. I'm going," Alasha said.

"Good girl. Up this way," Mamlith said, holding the squirming Brian tightly around his neck so that he couldn't talk, and forcing Alasha in front of him.

16

Worthy

"I pulled the sword out!" Yenny yelled triumphantly. "I heard the ground crack!"

"That was my back!" Paleo said. Yenny looked down and saw Paleo on the ground, his hand on his lower back.

"Master Paleo! Let me help you up," Yenny said as he bent down, but Paleo swatted his hand away.

"I don't need help like an old man. I'm fine!" Paleo said as he struggled up.

"Why can't we just blast everything down?" Yenny whined.

"Don't you dare," Master Paleo warned, wincing from the pain.

The atmosphere on Celestial Tower was the exact opposite of that in Shiroho City. The air was cool, wind shuffled through the trees, animals could be heard everywhere, and dark blue water was seen on the horizon instead of glowing red lava, waves crashing below. Both moons were visible, though the blue moon was still far larger, and so solid-looking that Yenny felt he could have touched it from where he stood.

"You never stayed up this late before," Yenny commented.

"You never needed my support this late before," Master Paleo replied. "When you rest, I will rest." The old man grasped his back and furrowed his brow. Yenny knew his master had pulled something while trying to help him with the sword.

"Let's rest," Yenny said. "Oh, yeah, I forgot to show you. Someone gave me an Elven Eye, but everyone told me it doesn't work." Going into his bag, he pulled out the Elven Eye. The brilliant orange orb stilled sparkled with light from the thousand stars floating in it.

Paleo's eyes dilated in delight. "Ah, it's authentic. A very rare item, made by the woodland mystics. Your friends probably didn't know you have to be a light or shadow astromer to make it work—unless you are an experienced krystee, of course. Since your own astromy makes it work, it's not going to properly show you places your eyes have never seen." Master Paleo took the orb from Yenny's hands and stated clearly, "Let's see . . . let's try Shiroho City."

The stars swirled rapidly in the crystal sphere. The vision within morphed into a city where a castle stood. Red and blue fireworks went off behind it.

"Wow!" Yenny said. "So the Elven Eye really does work! I should go back and tell Alasha sometime."

The moment Yenny said "Alasha," the orb shifted its view from the black castle to a patch of dark woods at the base of a nearby mountain.

"Wait a moment. That's Alasha and Brian!"

"Who?" Master Paleo asked.

"My two new friends from Vennisburg. Look, that man has a knife on them. Who is he?"

"Be quiet for a moment," Master Paleo said. He closed his eyes tightly, and the Elven Eye began to shake.

"Move it, girl," a voice echoed. "No funny business, or that'll be it for your friend here."

Yenny could have recognized that cold voice anywhere. "It's Mamlith!" Yenny said. "He's alive. He found Brian and Alasha. What if he's looking for the Fire Baetylus?"

Master Paleo looked at Yenny with concern and sighed deeply. "We can't do anything from here, Yenny. By the time we get there, he would already have the Baetylus. He'll be very powerful, maybe even more than me!"

"I know something that can beat him." Yenny jumped into the fire once more and pulled at the hilt of the sword. The flames swirled around him, and he was suddenly back in the now familiar underground chamber, but he did not hesitate. He gritted his teeth and pulled so hard he heard his shoulders pop.

"Why, if it isn't our favorite son," came Yenny's father's voice. Both of Yenny's parents again stepped forward out of the shadows, giant smirks on their faces as they watched Yenny struggle.

"You really think they'll believe you just because you have a sword?" said Yenny's mother, laughing.

"I can see through you into your heart," said his father viciously. "You want to replace us, do you? You think that boy and that girl can be your new family. You were never good at lying to your mother, Yenitus."

"Don't take our word for it, son," Yenny's mother said.

All at once, a choir of voices rang in Yenny's oversized ears: "You can never be king! You can never be king!" Yenny recognized several voices as the people of Vennisburg, including Professor Chaff. Over and over again they refused to acknowledge him.

"That doesn't matter!" Yenny yelled. "Someone needs to save Brian and Alasha!"

And suddenly, Yenny no longer stood in the underground

room. The voices disappeared. He was looking out over a rocky mountain, surrounded by the heat of a furious sun. Sweat glued his armor to his skin. He stood at a far greater height than usual, looking over an expansive battle raging at the mountain's foot. The valleys were full of flames, lightning, and smoke that rose to fill the sky. Motionless bodies were piled up in what looked like a small hill, and yet the battle hurried onward.

The sword was already in Yenny's strong, tough, bloody hands, because he had been crowned king long ago. He did not need to see his own face, for he knew who he was now. He was Day King Titan, the Krystee King.

"Do not be afraid," King Titan said with the sturdy tone of a true king. His deep voice was so commanding that Yenny was startled. But King Titan continued to speak. Yenny wondered if Titan sensed an intruder in his mind.

"Of course I sense you, Yenitus!" King Titan spoke out loud, his eyes not leaving the battle. "I know this was not what you have foreseen. But I have foreseen many things for you. The Night Lord has fallen, but his legacy has not. That is why I hid the sword not with stone, but with your own fears. I wanted you to struggle longer than I have, and gain more strength and humility than I."

King Titan turned away from the battle and walked toward a misty gray road; the lane was guarded by dead trees that moaned with agonized voices.

"Farewell. If I have succeeded, then I can finally walk the Strangers' Road and pass away. If I have failed, then you and I must meet in the flesh. Prepare yourself for my failure."

"You did it! Well done!" Master Paleo's voice broke the illusion.

Yenny was back on the tower, and his arm felt much heavier. He looked down and gasped. The sword! The same sword that Day King Titan had held in his vision, the sword that contained the power of Theo—Yenny had unlocked its power for the first time in two thousand years. He couldn't stop the thought: He was invincible!

"Well done, Yenny! Well done!" praised Master Paleo as he helped Yenny to his feet. "I knew the sword would come to you."

"Thanks," said Yenny. He looked around. He had expected a heavenly host to come down, or perhaps ocean and sky to switch places. But the sky did not open, and the sun, water, and wind were the same as before. "So was *nothing* supposed to happen? And what did I just see?"

But Master Paleo had already dropped to his knees and begun to whisper a prayer of thanks.

"Master Paleo, my friends are in trouble. They got captured, remember?"

But Master Paleo was in too much bliss to even notice. He was on his knees, his hands outstretched to the stars, giving thanks to each constellation and star he could name.

"I'm getting Supersonic Airmaster," Yenny said. He knew Master Paleo prayed forever when he was thankful.

Yenny had always hated heights, but like he'd trained himself, he closed his eyes and jumped off the tower. His shoulders bulged, and Yenny felt as though the bones in his back were rearranging themselves under his skin. Even after all this time, it felt uncomfortable as he heard his bones pop like bubbles and felt the muscles in his back loosen and spread to allow his wings to break through.

"Don't look down," Yenny repeated to himself. The

concentration of muttering helped him not to throw up. He soared down the stone steps faster than he meant to.

A shape blocked the sun. Unsuspecting of danger, hovering far off the ground, Yenny barely swerved away from four long claws—claws that protruded from the fist of a man wearing dark green armor.

In a flash of leafy color, the Raider fell past Yenny. Yenny wondered if they had made eye contact, and if so, what kind of eyes the Raider had.

The Raider landed on the water below, but astonishingly did not sink; the water around his feet puckered only slightly under his weight, as though he were standing on strong plastic. Yenny gazed down in disbelief, blinking several times to make sure he was seeing clearly. Walking on water was one of the oldest miracles, supposedly only performed by those who had achieved the highest levels of astromical spirituality, far beyond Master Paleo's wisdom. It seemed that theory had now been proven false.

Even from his great height, the Raider's claws looked sharp enough to carve steel, and Yenny knew he had only seconds to react. He glanced around for something to astromize, then made up his mind and concentrated. He brought forth a small forest from the seashore. The rising trees sent sand and water everywhere, and waves crashed underneath them. Yenny kept tripping in the slippery trees covered in seawater before conjuring a large cocoon of slithering branches to protect him from the Raider's blades and the water.

With a mighty *CRACK*, a metal hand pierced the wood cocoon and yanked Yenny out by the leg, digging painfully into his skin and hanging him upside down. Using a foot, the Raider pinned one of Yenny's arms to a branch. Then the armored man brought his claws close to his face.

A blast of intense light shined down on them, glinting off the Raider's armor. The light persisted only for the briefest moment, but the Raider slowed, and Yenny's krystee eyes caught it.

Yenny took his chance and waved his arms in wild circles, constraining the armored man's arms and legs with as many astromized vines as he could before kicking himself free and jumping away into the air. Above them, riding Supersonic Airmaster, Paleo descended on the Raider, his face focused and his glowing, outstretched hand ready to fire more beams of blinding light.

"Why spend all day pulling out a sword if you're not even going to use it?" Master Paleo asked as Yenny flew onto Supersonic Airmaster. From Master Paleo's arms, Fireworks barked in agreement.

"Let's just get out of here!" Yenny shouted. As Supersonic Airmaster's wings beat faster, Yenny dared to look back and glimpsed the Raider freeing himself. And then the Raider was gone.

Brian, Alasha, and Mamlith had reached the entrance to a dark tunnel, partly covered by trees. From the dingy depths came a wave of heat.

"Want to see something cool?" Mamlith asked. Without waiting for answer, he held out his free hand toward the entrance. A blast of light erupted from his palm, and the trees bent underneath it. "The mishap with the Light Baetylus wasn't a complete waste. The backlash fused some of its power to me. So, for example . . ." A blast of light propelled Alasha off her feet and into the wall of the mountain.

Brian gritted his teeth and struggled even harder.

"I don't think so, Boulard. I need you with me so that Miss Snowflake here will get the Fire Baetylus for me. I don't want to suffer the same fate as what happened with the Light Baetylus. Well, Alasha? Aren't you supposed to be leading us somewhere?" Mamlith asked.

It was clear Mamlith had explored this path already. "Left . . . . Right . . . . Climb," he commanded at every junction, with absolute certainty. "Move it," he yelled when Alasha slowed, out of breath from the climb. With each order, he shoved his knife against Brian's back to prevent either of the kids from making a move.

Mamlith's other hand continued to unleash the powerful light he had gained from the Light Baetylus weeks ago. Brian had to admit that even if they could find a way to escape, they would have nowhere to go without Mamlith lighting their way.

"Right across here," Mamlith said as they made their way to a rickety bridge painted with ash, leading across a great red chasm full of molten lava.

"That looks dangerous," Brian said.

"Hmm," Mamlith pretended to think. "You're right. We'll make the girl go first. Thank you, Boulard."

Alasha's mouth opened for a second, but whatever she was going to say was kept silent. She slowly led the way across, and Brian saw her legs shake as she stepped on each board. Brian's gut churned with nerves as he was pushed forward.

Soon they were surrounded by black, jagged walls, and air so hot that Brian's shirt was instantly soaked in sweat. Below, a fat, overflowing lake of lava was ready to catch anyone unfortunate enough to trip. Loud hissing filled Brian's ears, but he soon realized that the sound did not come from the lava. Giant lava serpents, better known as pypents, were thriving somewhere out of sight. They practically lived in the molten rock. To them, a warm, dry, stuffy summer day in Shiroho would feel barely above freezing.

Crossing the rickety bridge wouldn't have been a fun experience even if there hadn't been a fiery lake full of pypents at the bottom. The boards cracked with each step, and the slippery ash was worse than ice. Meanwhile, Brian kept stumbling under Mamlith's weight, as the man seemed to have a hard time walking with his injuries. Brian tried his best to keep his weight steady while they stepped one board at a time over the bridge; too much movement could have resulted in both of them falling over the edge.

"Not one sudden movement. Neither of you," Mamlith said.

They walked slowly onto the ledge. The last plank broke right as Brian stepped onto it, making Alasha squeal.

"I'm okay, young lady. I know you're just so concerned about me. Now kindly continue," said Mamlith.

Alasha led the way up the darkest, hottest tunnel yet, which was slippery with ash caked to the floor. Brian struggled to walk without slipping.

Soon a red light appeared above them, and they entered a large room where the walls were painted with murals that glowed as if they too were on fire. The murals showed dwarves hammering away through the mountains, looking for treasures.

"There she is," Mamlith whispered.

In the middle of the room, a pedestal stood alone, and on it was a large jewel. It was perfectly round like the Light Baetylus, but instead of white, it was a bright crimson. It was just *there*, not guarded by dogs or surrounded by wire. It seemed too simple to grab the stone—until Brian remembered that dwarves were well-known for building traps to protect their wealth. Supposedly, dwarven traps were the kind you didn't know existed until your fate was already sealed.

Mamlith may have been thinking along the same lines, for he said, "Grab the Baetylus, girl. You stay with me, Boulard. Just in case." Mamlith was looking around, and Brian was sure the man was curious what would happen if they picked the Fire Baetylus up.

Alasha walked toward the Fire Baetylus. The stone burned bright red, as though it had its own fire blazing inside. Brian hoped it wouldn't scorch Alasha's hand. She walked around the pedestal twice, looking for any trap that could harm her if she reached for the stone.

"Now!" commanded Mamlith.

Alasha breathed in deeply and touched the stone's surface. Nothing happened. With both hands, she snatched it up and quickly stepped away. Brian held his breath, but nothing happened—not a sound, besides Alasha whimpering.

"Good," Mamlith said happily. "Now give it to me, and then we'll discuss what happens next."

CRACK!

The carvings of the dwarves cracked to pieces, and lava burst forth from them. It looked as though they had triggered a trap after all.

Brian and Alasha just managed to avoid stepping into a puddle of lava, when they saw something just as bad. A gigantic lizard-like thing was squeezing its way out of a crack that had suddenly opened like a zipper in the black walls. It landed on the ground heavily and shook lava off itself, revealing purplish-black scales. Across the walls, more pypents were squeezing inside, drenched in lava. But then, Brian became more scared than he had been all night.

Mamlith charged at Alasha and jumped on top of her. Ignoring the pypents and the lava, Brian jumped onto Mamlith's back, tearing at the burned skin underneath his bandages. Mamlith screamed in pain, and the three of them wrestled each other to the ground until Mamlith let Alasha go and rolled away.

For a wild moment, Brian thought he had managed to fight Mamlith off—until he saw the Fire Baetylus clutched in the tyrant's scarred hand. A halo of fire swirled around it, and Mamlith used its power to cool the closest fountain of lava into unmoving stone.

"It's mine!" cried Mamlith. He raised the stone, and a massive wall of fire erupted from the Baetylus and spread across the vast ceiling.

Behind Brian, lava was approaching dangerously quickly. In front of him, the blind pypents finally started to crawl their way forward, snapping their powerful jaws. And beside him, Mamlith was spitting fire in all directions.

17

The Fire Baetylus

amlith's eyes glanced to his right, and he threw himself forward just in time. A pypent ran at him at full speed. He shot a great fireball at the nearest pypents, and several more circled around him.

Brian stepped in front of Alasha, ready to punch and kick at anything; but the two were completely ignored. In fact, the more fire Mamlith sent at the pypents, the more they ignored Brian and Alasha.

Mamlith was soon backed against a small pool of lava. Realizing he was cornered, he pointed the Fire Baetylus toward the lava. The stone glowed and cooled the lava instantly, but the pypents approached even more quickly, attracted to the heat and power of the Fire Baetylus.

That was when Brian realized what the trap was. It was a sadistic choice: burn alive in lava, or get assaulted by giant lizards. Using the Fire Baetylus to cool the lava had put Mamlith at the center of the pypents' attention. If he was to put the stone away, he would have to deal with the continuous flow of lava.

"Come on," Alasha said. She pulled Brian around the giant lizards, whose scaly tails almost knocked them into the rising pool of lava.

Mamlith launched a mighty fireball past them and scorched

the wall, which was the final bait. The pypents launched themselves with full force at Mamlith, who released blasts of white light to scare them off.

Brian and Alasha ran into the main tunnel, which was completely black without Mamlith lighting the way. But a second later, it didn't matter. Brian slipped on the ash and slid into Alasha, and down they went. It was like tumbling down a dirty, icy slide, with sharp rocks jabbing at their limbs as they bumped into the walls they couldn't see.

They landed in front of the bridge on the ash-caked floor, got up, and ran through the plume. More boards broke as they ran across the hazy chasm. They only barely made it to the far side before the volcano gave a mighty burp, spraying a million drops of lava onto the burning bridge.

Outside, lava was thickly streaming down the hill. Below, a gathering of guardians in leather coats bearing the Fire Falcon symbol were using astromy to calm the fires. Brian could just make out what looked like a man wearing a crown in the middle of the group. It was King Cindoran, standing next to the largest falcon Brian had ever seen. It was the size of a horse.

"HELP!" Brian yelled. "There's a crazy guy in there."

"Too late!" came Mamlith's voice over the wind. He was above them, riding what could only be a camazot.

The guardians who were fire astromers ran to the flames, picked up handfuls of fire, and threw them like baseballs at Mamlith; the ones who weren't astromers threw their spears. But Mamlith's flames were too much for them. He laughed before casting massive fireballs at them all. The fireballs exploded like grenades, sending the guardians flying through the air.

"Fly me up, Horus!" Brian heard Cindoran command.

The giant falcon was long enough for Cindoran to mount it. Launching into the air, Horus carried Cindoran to meet Mamlith on his own steed.

They flew circles around each other, Cindoran attempting to stab the camazot and Mamlith retaliating with fire. Brian grabbed Alasha's sweaty hand and dragged her away, and he felt the blaze of a blast aimed at Cindoran that just missed the king

"Couldn't have made it without you two," Mamlith yelled as he descended on his camazot. "I'll reward you by making your deaths quick. It'll only be a few very painful seconds." He held the Fire Baetylus directly over them, and from the stone, Brian heard the roar of a real dragon.

A bolt of light, not red but pure white, came from behind Mamlith and struck his shoulder. He howled in pain, and the camazot swerved to the right to avoid another blast of white light.

"Yenny!" Alasha cried.

A shape was descending from high in the sky. As it got closer, Brian could make out the faces of Yenny and Master Paleo flying on the lamassu.

"Yenny, you safe!" Alasha called.

"Not for long," Brian said, grabbing Yenny by the shoulder. "Do you have *any* idea how much trouble you got us into?"

Before Yenny could answer, a red light and a burst of heat exploded from somewhere behind them. Master Paleo jumped forward and surrounded them with a bubble of light. They felt the warmth of the red fire all around them, but the flames didn't penetrate the shield.

"I've had it with the lot of you. Good riddance to you all!" cried Mamlith on the other side of the flames. With the hand holding the Baetylus, he shot flames at Cindoran, preventing him from flying any closer on Horus.

"Alasha, do something!" Yenny screamed.

"Brian, do something!" Alasha screamed.

"Like what?" Brian yelled back, hugging Alasha.

Yenny looked from Brian and Alasha to the shaking Master Paleo, who was now practically on his knees, while Supersonic Airmaster screeched angrily. He looked at the steadily collapsing dome of light around them. Then he looked to the fancy sword he was holding. He looked as if he was trying to solve a very hard puzzle.

"What is that supposed to do?" Brian screamed—but it was too late.

Yenny threw the sword with all his might. The sword circled through the air toward Mamlith. The next moment, the fire that had surrounded them had vanished, and the great bat let out of high scream of pain. They saw Mamlith and his camazot fall toward the ground, the giant sword sticking out from the beast's side. Mamlith was so busy trying to stay on the camazot's back that the Fire Baetylus fell from his hand, far above the ground.

"Yenny, no!" Alasha screamed.

Yenny ran forward and jumped up, using his wings. In the air, he caught the Fire Baetylus with his left hand and stretched his right hand outward. Brian was not sure what he saw, but it looked like the sword was somehow pulled out of the camazot and flew into Yenny's hand. Yenny landed off-balance and fell to the ground. Nearby, Mamlith and the camazot fell crashed to the ground, Mamlith tumbling over its wings and falling onto his own back.

"Yenny!" Alasha screamed, running over. Yenny looked

perfectly fine. "Are you okay?" Supersonic Airmaster landed next to Yenny, and Paleo jumped down. He pointed his glowing staff directly at Mamlith, who looked like he was in so much pain he couldn't have moved if he'd wanted to.

"I'm not hurt, Alasha," Yenny responded.

"Yes, you are! You have flame welts on your body."

"Oh—I'm fine." Yenny turned red when Alasha touched his face, and he soon seemed unable to produce words.

"Alasha, this kid's—" Brian started, but something stopped him: He had taken his first look at the sword Yenny wielded. Yenny had always struck Brian as the type who would faint if he ever so much as picked up a knife. How had he gotten such a fancy, shiny new sword? "Where did you get that from?"

Before Yenny could answer, guardians approached from all sides to check on them. When they saw Yenny, they were shocked.

"He's a krystee?" a woman asked, pointing.

"A krystee?" repeated the guards. "Then you're Yenitus? The krystee boy who saved Vennisburg?"

"He says he's a king. I've read about him," another guardian said.

The murmuring gradually turned into applause, then into cheers that echoed through the burning streets. Just as in Vennisburg, Brian could tell no one believed Yenny to be a king of any sort, but a boy who had saved the day twice was good enough for them.

"Bring them inside!" commanded King Cindoran from directly above them.

The guardians formed a ring around the kids and their leader as they walked to the castle. All around them, people fought to break through to see who was special enough to need so much protection.

Yenny and Master Paleo walked inside first, while Brian and Alasha walked as slowly as possible past the two guards who had denied them entrance into the castle earlier, to prove who was in charge now. Grumbling loudly, the two guards shut the door— but all at once, there was a commotion on the outside.

The door guard stepped inside. "Apologies, my lord, but there is an individual outside who expressed interest in killing these two." The guardian pointed at Brian and Alasha, who looked worriedly at each other. "What should we do?"

"Bring the person in," Cindoran stated. "They could be linked to Mamlith." The guardian disappeared behind the door.

"It's okay," Brian said to Alasha. "Whoever it is can't hurt us here." The guardians quickly returned, grabbing the arms of someone who was struggling to get free. Yenny gasped.

Brian whipped around to see who the intruder was. "Never mind; we're dead," Brian said, and Alasha nodded.

Professor Chaff, sweaty and panting, still wearing her lab coat, stomped and kicked at the air around her as the guardians propelled her forward by the arms. She looked almost comical, until Brian saw a mad gleam in her eye that made him wish he was facing Mamlith again.

"You two!" Professor Chaff struggled, her finger switching from Brian to Alasha and back again. "RUNNING AROUND THE REGION WITH A RAIDER ON THE LOOSE—!"

"A Raider in *this* region? When?" asked King Cindoran.

"Save it. We need a Gaze Room, Cindoran," Paleo said. He was searching through his bag, and pulled out what looked like a roll of charts with star diagrams. King Cindoran led them past several hallways until they reached a large, mostly empty room with a glass ceiling.

"This looks like the room Mamlith had," Alasha said.

"Gaze Rooms are used for gazing at the stars," King Cindoran said, pointing at the sky. "Every major city is required to have one in the event that a saint shows up and need to make quick predictions."

"Quiet!" Master Paleo huffed, anxiously comparing his charts to the sky above him.

"How does that work?" Alasha asked, gazing upward.

"We look to see which stars are glowing brighter than the others," Professor Chaff said, still constrained; the opportunity to explain science made her forget her anger. "Kairos is the star that glows bright when something particularly important happens, something that has long-lasting effects."

"I said *quiet!*" Paleo said with a stomp. Everyone was silent for a moment, staring at the strange old man. Paleo took that as his cue to keep going.

For a while, the only noise was Horus, the giant falcon, clicking its beak against the floor. It made eye contact with Yenny and bowed its head. Yenny, blushing heavily, waved back.

"Yes!" Paleo burst at last. "You see that star, Kairos? It's the most important star we saints use. It's glowing brightly tonight, which only happens during key moments of fate . . . ."

"I *just* said that," Professor Chaff mumbled through her teeth. Cindoran waved at the guardians holding her, and they released her.

Master Paleo clearly didn't hear her. "And the three Great Constellations glowing brightly tonight are the Fox, the Swan, and the Elephant."

"I'm a fox!" said Yenny. "And Alasha and Brian are the other two!"

Paleo grabbed Brian and Alasha and pulled them forward to Yenny. "You three here together is what caused the stars to shift tonight. This is the sign we have been waiting for these past centuries."

"But how do you know it has to be us?" Alasha asked.

"Your three birth signs are shining between the Kairos, the star of destiny, and Zenith, the star of the Day King. This is why all of this happened the way it did tonight."

"And what, precisely, happened tonight?" Professor Chaff asked.

For the next hour, the company traded stories of what had happened on each individual adventure, starting with Yenny's first appearance in Vennisburg. All the tales answered everyone's questions about where Yenny had disappeared to, how he'd obtained his sword, and how Brian and Alasha had found the Fire Baetylus.

Alasha and Brian looked the worst of the group, covered in soot and scratches; yet they did most of the talking. "Yenny, let me hold the sword," Brian demanded after he'd had his say.

"No," Yenny said.

"I still can't believe you found Seirei," Professor Chaff said, her eyes wider than ever. She opened her briefcase; within it lay every sort of tool imaginable. "The fabled weapon that Day Kings use. It was lost for ages."

"I think so," Yenny said, holding the sword up higher to look at it. "It looks different from the one in the statue, though. Is it a mistake?"

"The sword takes on a different incarnation for every Day

King, each one unique to each King," Paleo answered. "When it was in the hands of Titan, it was known as Seirei, but now it is up to you to name your sword."

"How about . . . the Blade of Might?" Yenny suggested.

"That's pretty good," Master Paleo said. Then he grunted. "Never mind. That name was already taken by Day King Seraphos."

"This was the great weapon Mamlith wanted," said Alasha. She looked at Brian. "That proves it. Yenny is the Mandalah."

"That's exactly right!" Master Paleo confirmed, smiling.

"What do you think, sir?" Brian asked, hoping their nation's leader would notice him.

Cindoran closed his eyes and sighed, scratching the temple beneath his crown. Finally, he looked up at Yenny. "You're a hero, boy. No one can deny that. But to admit that you are a king is something I can't do."

"You don't believe me either?" Yenny said in a whimper.

"There hasn't been a Day King in two thousand years," Cindoran replied. "No one will believe until they see you carry the sword themselves, and even that won't be enough. The Seven Angeli of Tashu were assembled as a result of a king's absence. But if you are who you say you are, we are looking at one of the greatest events of our time. Saint Paleo, what do you think?"

"I think we should start with the basics," Master Paleo answered. "If the Day King has been chosen again, it makes sense to resurrect the tradition in its entirety, including all related customs—at least the ones that don't upset the civil laws of our present time. The sword was just the first step. The Day Kings then had to obtain a sense of responsibility and wisdom on their own. They had to go on an Exploration."

"An Exploration?" Brian asked. He liked where this was going.

"It was a rite of passage to the throne," Master Paleo explained. "Previous Day Kings had to gather the Baetyli from across the world and bring them together. Once the Exploration was complete, the Day King, regardless of age or race, was crowned king by Theo himself and blessed with infinite wisdom and power." Master Paleo paused while everyone took in his words.

"Why did they call it an Exploration?" Yenny asked.

"Because the task involves constant traveling, from city to city, through mountains and rivers, inside caverns and clouds, until all the Stones are found. One Adventure for each Stone."

"I am familiar with those facts," King Cindoran said. "It was long said and believed that anyone who collected all the Stones of Life would have the power to summon Theo himself to the world."

"I would not be foolish enough to say that any mortal could summon him," said Master Paleo, "but Theo does present himself in some form to anyone who collects all ten Baetyli and brings them together." He took a step closer to King Cindoran, his staff tapping the floor. "I believe it would be best if Yenny follows this same path his predecessors did, as opposed to inventing some new method for him to become king. Yes, I believe that is what is fated to happen. It is not luck that he already has the Fire Baetylus and the Light Baetylus. See how Theo has worked everything out. If Yenny collects all ten, Theo and all the stars in the heavens will declare Yenny the new king."

"But the final choice must be left to Yenitus himself," King Cindoran put in. "What do you say, Yenitus? It's your choice, boy."

All eyes were on Yenny and the Stones in his hands. In his right hand was the crimson Fire Baetylus. His left hand bore the pure white Light Baetylus. Each gave off its own feeble light from the power sealed in their opaque depths.

Yenny muttered something quietly.

"Speak louder, Yenny," Master Paleo urged.

"What if they don't believe me either?" Yenny said. "What if no one does?"

"Then you're going to keep going forward, with or without their support!" Master Paleo answered firmly. "And when you're crowned king by the First Star himself, they'll say, 'We believed in you the whole time.' That's when you'll have to remember who your real supporters are." Master Paleo placed his thumb to his own chest.

"Then yes," Yenny said more loudly, taking a step away from Master Paleo. He puffed his chest out. "I want to try whatever I can. I won't let you down, Paleo."

"Very well, boy. It's time for the Oath of Malpha. Saint Paleo?" Cindoran asked. Cindoran put his left hand over his heart and held out his right. Yenny did the same. "Repeat after me; do you understand?"

"Do you understand?" Yenny repeated.

Cindoran was lost for words for only a second, and then continued: "I hold myself to my word, given to the Eldest Father, that I, with acquiescence from the laws of the land and heaven, take these evidences of fire and light, not as extensions of my power or my will, but for the purpose of aiding my brothers and sisters under the sun; for we all, great or small, poor or rich, renowned or meek, are his children. If I abuse these evidences, may Malpha hide them from my hands forever. If I falter, may he protect me from my errors and put me back on the straight path."

It took two tries for Yenny to get it, but Cindoran seemed satisfied.

"As an Angelus, let me just add this. That blade on your shoulder—it is more valuable than gold, rubies, magic spells, anything you can think of. Extraordinary things have a way of happening to the one who holds this blade."

"It's just a sword," Brian interjected.

"This is the sword that ended the War of the Keys, slayed Night Lord Beelzelem, and even kept the Eldest Doom at bay. Never lose it; never let anyone so much as hold it. Once word gets out that the sword has been unsheathed, you will have much more to deal with than volcanoes and pypents. All the same, no Day King has performed his Exploration without the blessing or company of a saint." Cindoran turned his head and looked at the only saint present. "Saint Paleo?"

"Did you even have to ask?" confirmed Master Paleo. "You all mark my words: Great things will happen soon, and you will wonder how no one saw them coming. The four of us are in for a treat."

"Four of us?" Alasha said.

"You two are coming, too," Master Paleo said. "I have no idea what the cosmos are planning, but if your stars shine this brightly when Yenny reaches another Baetylus, then you three together are what will change the world."

"Well, the thing is, we're kind of stuck with her," Brian said, pointing at his professor. "Professor?" he asked. "Think of it this way: Don't you want two annoying teenagers out of your hair so you can do some research?"

Professor Chaff bit her lip and furrowed her brow. "I won't

stop you two from traveling with the wisest man this world has ever seen. But you had better bring back a natural item from every corner of the world you go to, and study it. And I want a well-written book about astromy procedures from every prestigious library you visit—none of those colored pages. And I'm going to quiz you when you get back."

"Then it's settled," King Cindoran said. "You are all in good hands. You'll be getting the best maps of the safest roads. I suggest walking only during the daytime to avoid wayward malkins."

"We walking?" Alasha asked. "We walking to all those places?"

"It's an Exploration, not a vacation," King Cindoran said. "Unless Horus wants to fly you all over the world himself. Do you, Horus?" The falcon looked at Cindoran and cawed twice; Yenny laughed. "Yes, Horus has a way with words," Cindoran said with a smile, before turning to talk to the guardians again.

"Who cares, really? I'll finally travel the world," said Brian.

"And I'll get to see tons of animals," said Alasha.

"And food!" Yenny said.

Far above and out of sight, an armored figure sat in the darkest shadows of the arches of the ceiling, memorizing everything he could about the krystee boy. There he was, eating sweets he had just pulled out of his pocket. How foolish of the boy to wander so openly, perhaps never guessing that the armored man would hunt him to the ends of the world.

The armored man took out a needle and lifted his mask slightly. Face still concealed behind his mask, he stuck the needle into his neck as he squeezed its green liquid into his body. It eased the pain greatly.

ABOUT THE AUTHOR

BRANDON LAYNE is native to Richmond, Virginia, where he attended Virginia Commonwealth University, graduating with a biomedical engineering degree and a minor in chemistry. Despite his scientific studies, Brandon has always been most passionate about creative writing. His other hobbies include poetry, playing piano and viola, dancing, photography, and performing on stage.